"You want the truth, Jesse? The truth is I don't like you at all," Betsy said indignantly.

His answer was to pull her into his arms. He knew she was saying, darn you, anyway, Jesse Kincaid, why do you know so much about me. "How disillusioning," he murmured in a husky voice, his smile telling her it was useless to struggle. His gaze roamed her face. From the look in his eyes, she knew exactly what he was thinking, feeling—and a wave of sensation rolled over her. She had to look away to avoid being sucked into the undertow. She felt naked. She felt as if she'd been scalded. She felt terrified at how easily this man could control her emotions, sense her needs.

When she could breathe again, she whispered, "Don't—"

"Too late!" He laughed and held her tight against his chest. "You like me, Betsy, and soon you're going to have to admit it. . . ."

WHAT ARE *LOVESWEPT* ROMANCES?

They are stories of true romance and touching emotion. We believe those two very important ingredients are constants in our highly sensual and very believable stories in the *LOVESWEPT* line. Our goal is to give you, the reader, stories of consistently high quality that may sometimes make you laugh, sometimes make you cry, but are always fresh and creative and contain many delightful surprises within their pages.

Most romance fans read an enormous number of books. Those they truly love, they keep. Others may be traded with friends and soon forgotten. We hope that each *LOVESWEPT* romance will be a treasure—a "keeper." We will always try to publish

*LOVE STORIES YOU'LL NEVER FORGET
BY AUTHORS YOU'LL ALWAYS REMEMBER*

The Editors

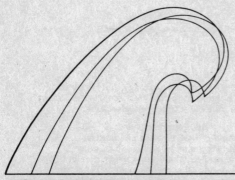

LOVESWEPT® • 205

Susan Richardson
A Slow Simmer

 BANTAM BOOKS
TORONTO • NEW YORK • LONDON • SYDNEY • AUCKLAND

A SLOW SIMMER

A Bantam Book / August 1987

If you would be interested in receiving protective vinyl
covers for your Loveswept books, please write to this address
for information:

Loveswept
Bantam Books
P.O. Box 985
Hicksville, NY 11802

ISBN 0-553-21831-X

Published simultaneously in the United States and Canada

Bantam Books are published by Bantam Books, Inc. Its trademark, consisting of the words "Bantam Books" and the por-
trayal of a rooster, is Registered in U.S. Patent and Trademark
Office and in other countries. Marca Registrada. Bantam
Books, Inc., 666 Fifth Avenue, New York, New York 10103.

PRINTED IN THE UNITED STATES OF AMERICA

O   0 9 8 7 6 5 4 3 2 1

One

Betsy Carmody looked from her son on one side of her
to her best friend on the other. Both were intent on the
football game. She sighed, brushed her dark chestnut
hair off her forehead, and lifted her face toward the
warm September sunshine. *Relax,* she ordered herself.
Tad and Olivia were enjoying themselves. She was going
to enjoy herself too, even if it killed her.

She closed her eyes behind her sunglasses and
breathed deeply, taking in the smells of beer and pop-
corn, hot dogs and mustard. Shouts and scraps of
conversation from the crowd around her blended into a
muted hum.

Now, this was nice. Wasn't this nice? she asked herself brightly.

It was no use. She opened her eyes and her gaze slid
sideways to her brown-haired six-year-old son. He was
leaning forward, his arms propped on the railing between field and front-row seats on the 50-yard line in
San Francisco's Candelero Stadium.

Football fever, she thought wryly, looking at Tad's
rapt, freckled face. A full-blown case. She supposed it
was inevitable. When your father had been Brian
Carmody, one of the best pass rushers ever to play in
the NFL, you had to be involved in the game. But she

didn't like watching it. Oh, Tad, she pleaded silently, be a librarian when you grow up.

When she saw Tad stiffen, she glanced at the field, and her gaze focused on the Miners' veteran quarterback, Jesse Kincaid. Somehow her eyes sought him out every time.

The announcer's voice came over the loudspeaker. *"Here's Kincaid, rolling out on the right side, looking for a receiver. No one's open, so he'll run it—No, he passes it to Collins."* The announcer's voice rose in glee. *"It's a flea-flicker pass, and it's caught the Rangers completely off guard. Collins is down on the forty for a gain of ten. Wow, that is pure vintage Kincaid, and the Rangers are frothing at the mouth."*

Against the swelling roar of the crowd, Betsy heard Tad and Olivia exclaim simultaneously, "Will you look at that!" She smiled. The words were identical, but the meanings, she knew, were worlds apart. Tad was impressed by Jesse Kincaid's athletic skill; Olivia was frankly interested in the quarterback's physique.

Betsy said teasingly, "If I'd known how much you'd enjoy this, Liv, I'd have brought you along sooner."

Olivia turned snapping black eyes on her friend. "If I'd known what was parading around on that field, you sure would have. Alex is going to have to fight me for the ticket from now on."

Olivia's teenage son Alex usually brought Tad to the game, using the lifetime season tickets that had been presented to Betsy as a gesture of sympathy when Brian had been killed in a car crash.

"It's a two-way fight, then," Betsy said. "I don't care if I never watch another body being carried off this field."

Olivia wasn't listening. "Just look at those shoulders!" She moaned.

"Olivia, do you think maybe it's time you remarried?" Betsy asked with gentle raillery.

"Introduce me to number seventeen and I'll consider it." Olivia pointed to the field, where Jesse Kincaid was huddled with his teammates, giving them the play.

Betsy's gaze followed Olivia's finger, and she studied the quarterback. Sweat-darkened golden-blond hair showed at the edges of his helmet. His tanned face was streaked with dirt. Talking and gesturing emphatically, he looked tough and intense. His eyes, Betsy remembered, were dark brown.

She could have introduced Olivia to Jesse Kincaid. Three years ago, he'd wanted to be her friend, but she wouldn't let him. She'd fiercely resented his kindness, because she knew what he thought of her.

There had been a fight in the locker room between Jesse and Brian, and the newspaper reporters had found out about it. When she asked Brian what had happened, he told her that the fight had started because Kincaid had called her a wet blanket.

Well, she admitted now, she had been a wet blanket. Brian had kept her so short of money that she couldn't afford nice clothes, and most of the time she'd been too unhappy even to smile. To someone as sophisticated as Jesse Kincaid, she must have seemed like a total drip. But he had been kind to her after Brian had died.

It still rankled.

She saw Jesse straighten up and slap one of his teammates smartly on the rump. The players trotted to their places, a band of warriors taking up battle positions.

You could tell how the game was going by the way the players moved, Betsy thought. If they were far behind, they walked slowly to the line. If they were well ahead, they walked briskly but calmly. If the game was hanging in the balance, they trotted, jumping into position and quivering with anticipation. They were professionals. Mercenary warriors.

Unlike his teammates, Jesse didn't trot. He never showed either eagerness or discouragement. Always the cagey general, Betsy remembered. Always thinking. The muscles in his thighs contracted in long ridges as he bent to receive the ball.

She swiftly looked away, annoyed at how her stomach muscles tightened when she watched Jesse Kincaid

move. It was revulsion, she decided. It couldn't be anything else. She disliked everything he stood for.

Her sexual attraction to a man had royally messed up
her life once. Looking at a gorgeous athlete would never
again arouse anything in her but distrust. She'd let
Olivia do the ogling.

And Olivia *was* ogling. She shook her head, setting
her short dark curls bouncing. "Forget marriage. I'll
settle for an affair."

"Most of them are boring and already married," Betsy
stated flatly. In an undertone she muttered, "Not that
that would stop a lot of them." It had never stopped
Brian. There'd been a girl with him the night his Porsche
had hit a telephone pole. The woman had lived.

Betsy could feel bitterness seeping through her, caused
by the painful memories that simply being at the game
dredged up.

She wouldn't think about it. Her eyes scanned the
stands, and she tried to focus her attention on the
crowd. Brian used to say, scornfully, that she was more
interested in the fans than the players. There was some
truth to that. She'd hated what Brian's brawling, show-
off style of play revealed about him, and she hated
constantly fearing that he might be seriously injured
and become a furious invalid for life.

Behind her a balding man in a Miners jacket shouted,
"Get six, Jesse! Get six!"

Betsy winced only slightly as beer from the man's
plastic cup sloshed onto the back of her seat. Olivia
watched her dab at the beer. "You look about as comfy
as Queen Elizabeth at a wrestling match," she said.

"Why?" Betsy asked defensively. "I'm having a wonderful time." In response to Olivia's disbelieving smirk
she added in a low voice, "Or I would be if they weren't
playing football down there."

"Right," Olivia drawled sarcastically. "There's no place
you'd rather be."

"Mom, can I have a hot dog?" Tad begged in his
piping voice.

Betsy rolled her eyes and groaned, reaching for her

wallet. "If you're sick during the night, don't call me," she commanded. The food was another thing she didn't love about sports events. The smell of sizzling nitrites alone was enough to keep her in her beautifully equipped cooking school among the avocados and goat's cheese.

To Olivia she murmured, "How can he eat this stuff. . . ."

"It won't kill him. Alex existed on fast foods before I met you."

Betsy shuddered. She handed Tad money and flagged down a vendor in the aisle. "I don't want to hear about it. I might have to fire you." Olivia grinned. Betsy could fire Olivia as easily as she would fire Tad. Without Olivia in the kitchen, the take-out end of Betsy's gourmet food business, which she operated out of her home, would collapse.

Besides, they were like family to each other. Alex was older brother and nephew to Tad and Betsy. Olivia was aunt and sister.

The loudspeaker crackled again. *"It's the Miners' hurry-up offense—they're going without a huddle to keep the Ranger defense off balance. Calling the signals is Jesse Kincaid. He hands off to—No, it's a play-action fake. He's looking for a receiver. The defense isn't fooled this time. They're after him in a pack. He's going to be sacked! They nailed him, throwing him for a loss of fifteen yards! Marlowe gets the credit for the sack!"* The announcer's voice was shrill with excitement.

Around Betsy a groan rose from the crowd and increased in volume as the quarterback lay motionless on the ground. "He's not getting up! He's hurt!" Exclamations punctuated the background murmur of fifty thousand voices. Betsy's eyes widened and her hand went to her mouth. Oh, no! Not Jesse!

Referees were pushing players away from the quarterback, who lay on the ground; Miners' trainers rushed onto the field and knelt beside him. Betsy bit her lip hard. *Please! Get up, Jesse!* she pleaded silently.

The stadium was strangely quiet. After several tense

minutes, Kincaid was helped gingerly to his feet. Betsy was able to breathe again.

"He's up," Tad said unnecessarily.

"That's a good sign," agreed Olivia.

Someone picked up the helmet that had been knocked off Jesse and held it out to him. He shook his head groggily and reached for it. Betsy's grip on the railing eased. "He's going to be all right," she murmured, watching him walk off the field toward the bench in front of their seats. He moved haltingly, but under his own steam.

Behind her a vocal fan shouted, "Roughing the quarterback! Give 'em fifteen yards!"

Another voice chimed in, "Fifteen yards, hell! Kill the so-and-sos." Everyone within earshot joined in the laughter.

"Kincaid's a popular man," Olivia observed.

"More than popular," Betsy said. "The fans think he walks on water." They had some reason for it, she mused. You could tell a lot about a man by the way he handled the pressures of a game.

Brian had been flamboyant, and the fans had loved him. He did little war dances over downed quarterbacks and taunted the offensive linesmen. Brian Carmody had possessed great entertainment value.

It was awe more than love that Jesse Kincaid inspired, Betsy reflected. He was colorful, too, but in a different way. His was a flamboyance of excellence. It showed in the way he routinely threw impossible eighty-yard passes, ran trick plays for the sheer fun of it, scrambled and danced his way around bulkier defenders, and read pass coverages and bypassed them. He had flair and verve, a gift for doing the unexpected. He was arrogant and he had a temper, but he was never obnoxious.

Even his off-the-field exploits had a different flavor from Brian's. Brian was arrested for drunk driving, with voluptuous ladies in the front seat with him; Jesse Kincaid was interviewed at opera openings, with socialites on his arm.

Still, there was enough similarity between the men to make Betsy recoil at the sound of Jesse Kincaid's name.

The crowd cheered as he left the field. He'd improved enough to slap the new quarterback on the back as the man went into the game, but his face was pale and strained. That must have been a painful hit he'd just taken, Betsy realized.

As Jesse limped to the bench, Tad cupped his hands around his mouth and yelled, "Way to go, Kincaid!"

Betsy was about to put out a restraining hand, then checked herself. Let him shout. Let him do the whole bit.

Jesse squinted upward against the sun, automatically seeking the source of that shrill voice. Things still looked a bit fuzzy, and there was a ringing in his ears. The crowd above him was a blur until suddenly one face jumped out at him in sharp focus.

Good Lord! It was Bettina Carmody, he thought in shock, struggling to clear his mind and his vision. He hadn't thought about her in months, and he'd forgotten how very much he liked her looks.

Her expression was anxious. He wondered why, and a flood of longing overwhelmed him. *I wish it were for me,* said a voice from deep within himself.

Betsy saw Jesse stiffen like a hound scenting a bird. His eyes widened, then narrowed as he stared at her. He nodded a slow greeting.

She looked away, horrified to feel blood rush into her cheeks. She hadn't blushed in years! Would she ever outgrow it?

Jesse's pain receded as Betsy claimed all his attention. Mentally, he whistled. Whew! What had she done to herself? He had always liked looking at her. Her rich chestnut hair had framed a delicate roses-and-cream face and fallen down her back, almost to where her long, lovely legs began. A wild colt, he thought, surprised at how vividly he remembered her from three years before.

And now! Damn, she was beyond beautiful! She'd

cut her hair to shoulder length. The style gave her a poise and sophistication she'd lacked before. Was it just her hair and clothes that made the difference? he wondered, noting her tailored shirt and green linen jacket. No, he decided. There was something different about the entire set of her head and shoulders. Somewhere along the line she'd acquired confidence. Her mouth, once soft and innocent looking, had firmed.

He felt a surge in his midsection, but he couldn't stop staring. Just in time to keep him from making a fool of himself by approaching her during a game, the final buzzer sounded. The Miners had won.

Pandemonium broke loose, with fans clapping and yelling and streaming onto the field.

Jesse allowed a concerned trainer to help him into his silver-and-gold Miners warm-up jacket, then shook off several importunate fans and made his way toward Betsy.

"He's coming this way!" Olivia whispered excitedly.

"Mom, look!" Tad exclaimed.

Betsy looked—at a face and expression she remembered from three years ago. This time Jesse was gazing up instead of down at her. His brown eyes were warm, his smile assessing. Her heart began an uncomfortable thumping while her spine stiffened.

His hands were jammed into his pockets. He looked huge up close. His shoulders, emphasized by the pads, were enormous. On the field, he seemed tall but slim next to the barrel-chested bulk of many of the players.

"Hello," he said in his rich baritone voice. He nodded again and tried to gauge her resistance from her posture. She'd always resisted him. He wished she'd take off her sunglasses. "How are you?" he asked.

Around them people jostled Betsy and called out to Jesse, some stretching out their hands to touch him. But for the two people rediscovering each other, the crowd didn't seem to exist.

Betsy watched the slashes in Jesse's cheeks deepen to long dimples as he smiled. He was still pale, but all his faculties were apparently working now. His crinkling eyes were uncompromisingly intelligent. They'd always made her uncomfortable, she remembered. He was a hard man to hide from.

She had to swallow before she could answer him.

"I'm fine, Jesse," she said, her voice a little husky. "You?"

"As well as I could expect after being trampled by elephants." His lips turned upward in an ironic smile. "You haven't been around in some time." That was an understatement. "It's good to see you, Bettina."

And it was good to look at her, he added silently, at her hair, which glinted with red highlights, and the sweet, sensitive curve of her mouth.

" 'Bettina?' " Tad parroted in disbelief.

"That *is* my name, honey," Betsy said mildly.

"What do you call her, young man?" Jesse asked the brown-haired boy.

"Mom," Tad replied guilelessly.

Jesse laughed. "Dumb question, huh?"

Betsy smiled crookedly.

"I call her Betsy," Olivia gushed, carefully avoiding looking at her friend.

" 'Betsy,' " Jesse said thoughtfully. "I like that."

"This particular fan of yours is Olivia Hart," Betsy said.

"Glad to meet you, Olivia."

"Me too," murmured Olivia.

Jesse turned back to Betsy. "I tried to find you after you moved three years ago, but you just disappeared. I'd like to see you again."

Betsy's lips parted nervously. He had forgotten about the tiny gap between her front teeth. It was the only thing that kept her from being a classic beauty. In Jesse's mind, it increased her appeal.

"Life goes on," she said somewhat breathily. "I've been busy with new things."

He smiled slowly. "But there's nothing like old friends."

"Except maybe new ones," Olivia said reproachfully.

"I teach cooking classes," Betsy explained, "and Olivia and I run a gourmet fast-food business called Calcuisine. It takes up most of our time."

"Impressive," Jesse said, nodding. "But you always were a good cook, as I recall."

What he recalled was that once she'd almost poisoned the entire team with overaged deviled eggs. Word had gone around that she'd enrolled in a culinary institute after that particular potluck dinner. He grinned wickedly at the blush that scalded her face. So she still blushed.

"Imagine your remembering that," she said in a silken voice.

"You'd be amazed at what I remember about you."

He watched curiously as her chin lifted. His remark had a different meaning for her than for him, evidently.

"I rarely think about those days, myself," she said coolly.

"No," he agreed. "You wouldn't."

Regret at being associated with the worst moments of her life swept over him. He'd often wondered if it would have been different between them if he hadn't known her during her disastrous marriage and the horror of Brian's death. If he'd met her first, maybe. In spite of her aloofness in those days, he'd always thought there was a bond between them.

"Well," she said briskly, rising to her feet, "you probably want to hit the shower."

To keep her from leaving, Jesse turned to Tad. "You've grown," he said, taking in the boy's big hazel eyes and engaging smile. "The last time I saw you, you were about two feet high." Tad gaped at him.

"You're going to be a big man," Jesse added, "like your dad."

Tad's eyes widened further. "You knew my dad?" he asked wistfully.

Betsy's heart turned over. Jesse must have felt something, too, for his voice softened as he said, "I sure did. He was quite a football player."

Tad sighed, completely happy. Jesse smiled in sympathy and amusement. He'd started the conversation to keep Bettina there, but his motive now changed.

"Would you like to come down to the locker room with me and meet some of your dad's old friends?" he asked.

Tad couldn't answer. His eyes got so big, they almost popped out of their sockets. Betsy felt her own eyes growing moist.

"Okay, Bettina?" Jesse asked, looking at her searchingly.

Darn, she thought. Nothing good could come of this. But she'd cut her throat before she'd say anything to take the ecstatic look off Tad's face. She nodded once, stiffly, then said gently to Tad, "Go ahead, Pole."

Jesse raised his arms over the railing and lifted Tad down. "We won't be long," he said reassuringly to Bettina. Then smiling whimsically, he added, "Sorry I can't invite the two of you as well."

"Me, too," Olivia sighed.

Jesse and Tad hadn't gone five steps when Jesse stopped, said something to Tad, and walked back to Betsy. While she looked questioningly at him, he reached up and casually removed her sunglasses. She gasped in astonishment.

He stared intently, as if he were searching for something.

He was. Her warm hazel eyes with their thick, sooty lashes were familiar. He recognized the clear directness in her gaze, and the wariness. He'd always felt that beyond her reserve, there were unfathomable depths to her. He wanted to find out what was down there. He'd always had an inkling that it might be something he'd been looking for for a long time.

Betsy felt pinned by Jesse's intense scrutiny. She couldn't look away. Her heartbeat sped, and she was catapulted into a place of heat and pounding blood.

Jesse smiled slowly as he carefully folded the glasses and handed them to her. "The better to see you with, my dear," he said softly, his meaning unmistakable. He turned and rejoined Tad, leaving Betsy staring and Olivia shaping her mouth into a soundless whistle.

As Betsy absently put the glasses away in her shoulder-bag, she noticed her hands were trembling. "Darn the man," she whispered to herself.

"You didn't tell me you knew him," Olivia said accusingly.

Betsy looked at her friend with bewilderment. "Well, of course I do. He was here when Brian was on the team."

"But you *know* him," Olivia insisted. "He talked as if you were friends."

"Hardly that," Betsy murmured, "but football players are people, you know, not gods. They have neighbors and acquaintances like everyone else."

"Casual acquaintances don't look at each other as if they've been struck by lightning."

"You're imagining things," Betsy said lightly. She pretended interest in the people streaming across the field, but Olivia was right. She knew Jesse Kincaid. She didn't want to. Her memories of everything to do with professional football should have faded, but she remembered Jesse Kincaid smiling down at her as if it were last week.

Olivia was right about another thing. Something had passed between her and Jesse just now. She knew sexual interest when she saw it. And for a moment, when he'd beamed it at her, she'd felt like she was going to faint. Then blood had rushed to her head, and she had been swimming in molten lava.

You fool! she told herself. The first time she'd felt that way she'd had an excuse. No one like Brian had even looked at her before. But surely now she'd seen enough handsome men not to swoon when one gave her a casual nod!

She was furious with herself and, in consequence, with him. *Just keep your hellos to yourself, Jesse Kincaid!* she said silently. *Keep out of my life! I didn't need your pity three years ago, and I don't need your admiration now!*

Two

After Jesse returned Tad to his mother and watched her beat a hasty retreat, he headed for the training room, thinking maybe he had a concussion. He felt like he'd been hit by more than a few defensive backs.

"Ready for some ice, Jess?" asked George, the head trainer.

Jesse grinned at George's cheerful face. "Yeah. My neck feels like hardening concrete. Besides, I could use a dose of cold reality."

He sat down, propped his elbows on his knees, and placed his head in his hands, while George applied ice to his neck. When he closed his eyes, he could still picture Betsy in his mind.

Her eyes and her mouth. He'd spent more time thinking about them than he'd had any right to. He'd hated it that she'd been married to a lout like Carmody. He and Brian had actually fought over her once, after Brian had complained about having to go home and curl up with his "wet blanket."

If Brian had lived, Jesse doubted that Betsy would have stayed with him, even for Tad's sake. Anyone could have seen she was miserable. She'd been unsure of herself then, but she was no masochist. Of that he was positive.

He had tried to help her after Brian died, often making excuses to drop by her house. She had been polite, but cool. Eventually he stopped visiting her. What could he do about a new widow who reje ted common courtesies? He never fully admitted to himself that he was offering more than condolences.

But now he was seeing Betsy as clearly as if she were sitting in front of him, and he asked himself why. She looked wonderful, and his mind was full of images of her with her hair messed up and her mouth softened and parted. He groaned, and George asked solicitously, "Too cold, Jess?"

"Not cold enough," he muttered. He wondered if she would try to freeze him out of her life this time, and if her skin felt as smooth as it looked. He decided he'd better wait awhile before calling her. A week, if he could stand it that long.

On the way home, Tad described every detail of the locker room and repeated every word that Jesse Kincaid had uttered. Betsy listened patiently.

"And when Jesse"—it was Jesse, now, not Kincaid—"put me on a bench and said who I was in a loud voice, whole bunches of these huge guys came over to shake my hand. Just like I was an important grown-up! There was one called Buster Brown." He looked confused when his mother and Olivia laughed, but was too excited to stop. "And one called Hap Tanner, who has a kid my size. And one sorta smaller guy named Coach." Running out of steam, he thus dismissed the man the press called the Einstein of the Gridiron.

"Well, you know, Tad," Betsy said, "size isn't everything."

"No," the boy agreed readily, "it's how tough you are too."

Betsy sighed in resignation. Olivia laughed, then asked, "Are you going to be tough, Tad?"

Her fatuous remark earned a disgusted look from

Tad, and he subsided into a corner of the car to relive his glorious day.

In an undertone, Betsy said to her friend, "I'll tell you what's going to be tough, undoing the damage that man did today with his flashing white teeth."

"Damage to Tad or to you?" Olivia asked slyly.

Betsy gave her a threatening look. "Don't project. The drooling was all on your side."

"Not all on mine. Some of it was being done by number seventeen. He thought you were good enough to eat."

"His kind don't eat women, they just chew them up and spit them out. A primitive form of pureeing."

Olivia rolled her eyes, snorting softly. "He can gnaw on my bones any old time."

"Olivia!"

"Just tell me what it is about him that gets your back up like this! It's not a normal female reaction."

"That's just it. He's too good-looking."

"Too good looking." Olivia nodded sagely. "Ah. That explains it."

Betsy grinned. "Too good looking, too virile, too everything. You can't trust your instincts around men like him."

"I don't know about you, but I trust mine fine," Olivia said suggestively.

Betsy briefly lifted her hands from the wheel in a gesture of resignation. "I give up."

"You do that. It's not much of a contest anyway. I'd cast him as the persistent type."

"You'd be wrong," Betsy said slowly. "If he's interested in me, it's because I'm one of about five people who don't gush over him."

"No other reason?" Olivia teased.

Betsy shook her head. "What else could there be?"

Olivia gazed at her friend curiously. "Have you looked in a mirror recently?"

Betsy waved a dismissing hand. "There are better-looking women on every block."

"I'd slit my throat if I thought that were true," Olivia stated.

Betsy wrinkled her nose fondly at her friend, who was pert and peppery, but definitely not beautiful. "You've got charm, sweetie. That's far better than beauty."

Olivia snorted grumpily in reply. Betsy grinned and concentrated on easing her way into the stream of traffic on the freeway.

It wasn't false modesty that made her doubt that Jesse Kincaid's interest in her would outlast the hour. She knew she was attractive, now that she'd found the style to carry off her height and slimness. She also knew she was no sex goddess. Brian had made that clear.

At first he'd thought she was pretty and had enjoyed her adulation. He'd been among the first of several men to notice her at Ohio State, when her coltish build had filled out and she bloomed into a startling, unusual beauty. But he'd been the only one with sense enough to become her buddy before he tried to become her lover.

Betsy, bewildered by the unfamiliar attention and dazzled by handsome, happy-go-lucky Brian, had sailed into marriage with her first true feelings of self-confidence.

When Brian's tendency to pout and snarl destroyed both her infatuation and her self-confidence, he turned back to the vivacious beauties who were more his type. Betsy had endured his infidelity as as long as she could, for Tad's sake. She was on the verge of leaving Brian when he was killed.

She had pulled herself together and started a new life, but it had taken her three years to rebuild her sense of self-worth. And some part of her still felt like Brian's wet blanket.

No, she was no centerfold. Betsy doubted very much if she'd hear from Jesse Kincaid again. And that would be fine with her. It would save her the trouble of brushing him off.

• • •

The following Friday Betsy followed her regular escort, Garrett Phillips, as he elbowed a path through the opening-night throng in the foyer of the opera house.

"Excuse me. Excuse me, please," Garrett said repeatedly. He wasn't forceful enough to make rapid headway, but finally they gained a measure of breathing room beside a Doric column.

Something had gone wrong, Betsy thought, gazing around. The foyer and the wide steps outside were a solid mass of rainbow satins, gleaming furs, formal black tuxedos, and glittering jewels that flashed as they caught the light. But the inside doors were shut, so no one could move more than a few steps.

"I'm sorry about this, Bettina. Can't imagine what's happened." Garrett was a conscientious man, and he seemed to be taking personal responsibility for the foul-up.

"I heard someone say something about the lights in the orchestra," Betsy said. "I'm sure they'll have it fixed in a minute." She smiled reassuringly at Garrett. "Don't worry. It gives me a chance to study all the gowns firsthand. That's half the reason I come, after all."

Garrett looked around abstractedly. "I think I might be able to make my way to the bar. Would you like a sherry or something?"

"That would be lovely," she said, more because Garrett seemed anxious to make up for the delay than because she wanted a drink.

"I won't be long." He waded into the crowd again.

Betsy relaxed against the column and prepared to enjoy herself. She was one of a few who were doing so, she realized. The place was agrowl with indignant remarks.

She wondered, not for the first time, if Jesse Kincaid would attend this opening. He was usually photographed at first nights. She supposed the idea of a football player having an interest in opera was bizarre enough to be news. She was just wondering, she told herself with a firming of her lips, not hoping. It didn't make any difference to her where Jesse Kincaid chose to make his appearances.

Jesse was no more than ten feet away from Betsy, and he was bored to death. And when he was bored, he was unpredictable. His teammates would have recognized the look in his eyes, but none of them was there to warn the members of the press prowling through the crowd.

At his side stood a beautiful brunette in a sequined red gown and white fur wrap. "I don't know why we bothered arriving late, Jesse, she said. "We haven't avoided the crush at all." She sounded rather pleased. Linda Ralston was an aspiring actress, and it was good publicity for her to be seen with Jesse Kincaid.

Jesse's mouth twisted. "Evidently not," he agreed, looking down at her and wondering why she wore so much makeup. The sleeve of his tux sported stripes of different colored eyeshadow. He realized he couldn't remember what color her eyes were. Not hazel, certainly.

His eyes narrowed as several small explosions of light announced the presence of photographers. He'd come late, feeling he could do without publicity pictures just now. Betsy might see them and draw the wrong conclusion.

Betsy's reaction had figured in most of Jesse's recent calculations. He hadn't been able to stop thinking about her. He'd been getting tired of Linda anyway, but seeing Betsy again had killed any remnant of interest he'd had in the actress. Every time she opened her mouth he compared her voice unfavorably to Betsy's soft, husky tones. Every time her teeth gleamed in a smile he found himself thinking about the shape of Betsy's mouth.

He would have avoided the opera altogether, except that Linda had been counting on it for weeks. Oh, well. He supposed he owed her that much, but it would be a farewell gift. He was tired of being used to further her acting career, and he was eager to clear the decks.

A flash unit held high above the crowd pointed in his direction. "Smile for the cameras," he said cynically.

Linda squealed in pretended protest, then said, "Might as well make it a good one." Standing on tiptoe, she grabbed Jesse's head and brought his mouth down to hers. Rage ricocheted through Jesse as the light flashed.

The flare drew Betsy's attention. With a little shock of recognition she saw Jesse, his face furious, impatiently push away a stunning dark-haired woman. At an angle across his tight mouth was a smear of lipstick, like a recent wound. With two strides he parted the crowd and relieved a gabbling photographer of his camera. With a sweep of his arm and a gleam of exposed celluloid, he returned the camera to the still protesting newsman.

Betsy heard a thin wail across the babble of sound in the lobby. "Who do you think you are? You can't get away with that!"

She didn't hear Jesse's answer, but his mouth clearly shaped the words, "Sue me!" Around him people edged away as if he were a dangerous lunatic.

Betsy's heart was pounding as hard as if she'd been involved in the fracas herself. Jesse's entire body radiated power and menace. At an ultra-civilized occasion like the opera, the little scene was shockingly incongruous.

In a tuxedo and starched shirt, Jesse Kincaid could play the role, Betsy thought, but he wasn't a civilized man. He'd be bound by conventions only as long as it suited him.

As if her fascinated face were a magnet, Jesse's head swiveled. His eyes blazing, he fastened his gaze on her as her own eyes widened in shock. She saw his lids descend in dismay, as if to block her out, then fly up as he found her again.

Damn! he thought. He'd gone to a lot of trouble to avoid publicity tonight, for her sake, and she was right on hand to see him at his worst. Of all the rotten luck! She looked as if she'd seen a ghost. Bullying photographers was probably something her late husband had specialized in.

The doors were open now, and the crowd began to move. Betsy stayed where she was, watching Jesse gravely. Garrett hadn't returned and she was in no hurry to enter that surge of tightly-pressed bodies.

Jesse's gaze never left hers. It was no trouble for him to make his way through the crowd, since he was used to battling bigger bodies. Face to face with her, he halted, forming a wall between her and the crowd. His date, swept on by the crush of people, didn't realize that Jesse was no longer behind her.

" 'Evening, Betsy," he said through taut lips.

"Hello, Jesse." She looked warily up at him, fighting to conceal the internal trembling that seemed to afflict her whenever he got too close. What was it about him that affected her this way? She should despise him, right? she asked herself. He'd just been rude and thoughtless to his date and abominably arrogant to the poor photographer. What she thought of him, however, seemed to have no effect on the way he made her feel.

Aloud she wondered, "Was the picture that much worse than fifty others? Why attack that particular photographer?"

A muscle clenched in Jesse's cheek. "His timing was off," he said baldly. "I was trying to present a pure image this month, to impress you."

Her eyes widened and she glanced quickly away from his intent brown gaze. She felt like a doe in hunting season.

"I guess I could have saved myself the trouble," he added wryly.

She glanced up to see him smiling humorlessly. Contrarily, she was amused. "You might say *your* timing was off." The slashes in his cheeks deepened into dimples as he smiled. Betsy watched, fascinated. He should be required to register his smile as a dangerous weapon.

"It was and it wasn't." He stared at her in a bold

challenge. "At least it got your attention. Two meetings in one week. We must be entering a new phase in our relationship."

"Quite a coincidence," she murmured.

"More of a portent, I promise you. Why don't we trade dates?"

She smiled briefly. What an outrageous flirt he was. His mouth sported another woman's lipstick, and he spouted come-ons.

"Mine's perfectly acceptable, thank you, but I think you may have lost yours." She peered toward the stairs at the opposite end of the foyer, where Jesse's date, realizing she'd been abandoned, was beginning to struggle back against the tide of people. She didn't get far before a reporter-photographer team stopped her to request a picture and ask a few questions.

A muscle twitched in Jesse's cheek again. He wished Linda were on the moon. "I'm not seeing her again," he said bluntly. "I want to see you."

Heat rose to Betsy's cheeks, and she stiffened, raising her eyebrows delicately. "You discard women like used tissues. Are all football players like that? Is it included in the job description?"

Jesse's eyes flashed in annoyance. Everything he said or did seemed to present him in a negative light. This was one of those situations where he was damned if he acknowledged Linda and damned if he denied her.

"You don't understand," he said urgently. "I'm part of Linda's agent's publicity schemes, nothing more. She won't miss me."

Betsy shook her head in mock admiration. "That's right. I'd forgotten how people in your line of work use one another."

"You're twisting things and you know it," he said, frowning. They stared at each other, deadlocked, until Jesse sighed and ran a hand through his hair. His face and voice softened. "Betsy," he said, smiling, "the last thing I want to do is argue with you. We were almost friends once. If we can't do better at the moment, why can't we at least start there?"

Betsy got her answer to his question from her body's response to him. He interfered with her breathing. He was absolutely the most attractive man she'd ever seen, and she doubted if he was capable of a platonic relationship with a woman other than his mother.

Time stretched thin while their gazes remained fixed and their minds raced.

Jesse thought Betsy's face was the most satisfying thing he'd ever seen. It was all clean, delicate lines and subtle colors. Without volition, his gaze roamed over the slim silver satin gown she wore under her pewter-colored velvet jacket. "You look like an icicle," he said, breaking the mood between them.

At Betsy's breathless laugh, he added, "That was a compliment. I meant cool and lovely. You make all these sequined and furred women seem overheated and overdecorated."

Her lips curved impishly as her gaze was drawn again to the red mark across Jesse's mouth. "You look like a war casualty."

Following her glance, Jesse touched his mouth and his hand came away tipped with red. "Damn!" he said softly and explosively. "You mean I've been pitching my lines all this time with this on my mouth? No wonder I'm getting nowhere."

She smiled, impressed. He was embarrassed, but he could see the funny side of it.

He pulled out a handkerchief and swabbed at his mouth. "Is it all off?"

"No, there's some in the left corner still."

"Would you get it?" He held the soiled cloth out to her.

She hesitated, not from fastidiousness, but from reluctance to involve herself in such an intimate situation with him.

"Please," he said. "It's just a matter of time before another photographer catches me."

She bit her lip and accepted the handkerchief. With businesslike motions she dabbed at the corner of his mouth, trying to distance herself from the action. He was so close she could see the tiny nick where he'd cut himself shaving, and she could feel the warmth of his breath.

His firm lips parted slightly, and breathing again became difficult for her.

Jesse was caught up in cataloging the kaleidoscope of colors that made up her hazel eyes. Betsy had a knack for making him forget crowds. His hand closed around her wrist. Under his caressing thumb her pulse raced. Her eyes shifted to his and darkened. They stared, both of them caught up in something beyond their understanding.

Another light exploded. Betsy saw fury in Jesse's expression before he whirled toward the source of that flash. She clutched a handful of his jacket and was carried forward a step when he lunged, before her weight slowed him.

"No!" she said urgently. "Jesse, let it be!"

His head swiveled around and he looked at her in disbelief. "You don't mind?" he asked incredulously.

"Of course I mind! But less than I'd mind another scene. Leave it, please!"

His mouth twisted as he stared beyond her at the photographer who was making good his escape. "What a farce!" It wasn't clear to Betsy if he meant the photographic episodes or his entire encounter with her.

There was no time to find out. The top of Garrett's blond head appeared in the stairwell, and Linda arrived, breathless and glaring from Jesse to Betsy and back again.

"So here you are, Jesse," she said with poisonous sweetness. "You've found a friend. Aren't you going to introduce me?"

"No," he said abruptly, reversing Linda's direction with his hand on her upper arm. "Let's take our seats." Over his shoulder he nodded a good-bye. "I'll be seeing you, Betsy. They say good things come in threes."

"How about bad things?" she murmured in self-defense.

His lips tightened, but he left without speaking.

At the stairs leading to the box seats, he turned and watched as Betsy accepted a wineglass from a tall, smooth-haired man. He felt he'd kill for a smile from her as warm as the one she gave her date. Bleakness settled over him as he followed Linda up the stairs. He barely heard her recriminations.

Three

The next day Betsy's phone rang for the tenth time. She turned off the mixer and snatched the receiver from its hook. "Hello," she said, forcing patience into her voice.

"Bettina? It's Jesse."

Her stomach jolted. It was one thing to encounter him in public; it was another to hear his voice right here, in her kitchen.

"Bettina? Are you there?"

"Yes. Hello." If she sounded abrupt, she couldn't help it. She wanted him off the phone before she did something stupid, like sound friendly.

"I'm calling to see if you'll have dinner with me tonight."

"No."

Jesse paused. Then, surprising her with his ready acceptance of her brisk rejection, he said, "All right. Can I speak to Tad then?"

"No." Her hand gripped the receiver. Her only defense against his strong, confident voice was rudeness.

But he didn't check at her response to his second request either. "Why not?" he asked reasonably. "Doesn't he like me?"

Betsy couldn't help but laugh. Why couldn't he be

offended, like a normal person, and hang up and leave her alone? She wiped her hand on her white chef's apron, then ran her fingers through her hair. "He idolizes you, as you well know, since you went to some trouble to produce that effect."

Jesse didn't deny it. "What then? I'm not a fit person for him to talk to? Is that it?"

"No. . . ."

There was enough hesitation in her tone to imply a different answer. "That *is* it. Why don't *you* like me, then?"

She sighed in exasperation. This was a ridiculous conversation! "It's not that. Not anything personal. I just don't want Tad any more football-mad than he is already. I want him to find out that there's lots more to life. And to be quite honest, I don't like football or football players." There, she thought. Let him have the whole truth, if a hint wasn't enough.

Gravely, he said, "Well, that's a reasonable, balanced position."

Another unwilling laugh gusted out. "I don't have to be reasonable."

"True. You can set any kind of parental example you want."

"Oh, shut up!" she snapped. "Why am I talking to you?"

His voice betrayed a smile. "It's that polite, responsible streak you haven't quite conquered." Then, giving her no time for a comeback, he said, "I'm the oldest quarterback in the NFL. I'll probably retire next year. Can we make a date for then?"

She laughed again. "Thirty-six years old, isn't it? A real fossil."

"Thirty-seven. And football's a young man's game."

"You'll never retire. You're indestructible. Everyone says so."

"I may be forced to," he lied cheerfully, "if you won't see me any other way."

She sighed heavily and tapped impatient fingers on

the telephone. "Look, Jesse, I'm going to hang up now. I'm in the middle of a soufflé."

"Sounds messy," he murmured. "Wait, Betsy."

It was unfair of him to call her Betsy, she thought. She held the phone an inch from her ear, irresolute.

"You're making me into a liar," he said. "I promised Tad I'd phone him."

She counted to ten silently. "You're just using him to get to me."

"You flatter yourself," he replied promptly. "And underestimate him. Tad and I have interests in common."

"Such as?"

"I'd say *you*, but if I did you'd hang up. . . ."

"Right."

"So I'll say sailing."

"Sailing?" she echoed incredulously.

"That's right. One of those things in life besides football. I promised him I'd take him sailing on the bay."

Her mouth set in stubborn lines. "No soap."

His tone was serious. "Bettina, I like him. He's a great kid."

Oh, he was so unfair.

He knew he had her. "I didn't have a father either, you know. He reminds me a lot of myself."

"If he needs a surrogate father, I'll get him one. And it won't be a football player!" she shrieked wildly.

He chuckled. "I'll be by to pick him up at two this afternoon, okay?"

"I'm not going to see you, Jesse."

"Oh, yes, you are," he said softly. "But that's a separate issue. I'll be by for Tad at two."

She was suddenly suspicious. "You don't know where I live. And how did you get my private number? It's supposed to be unlisted."

"I have spies in high places," he murmured mysteriously, then hung up.

Betsy stared at the dead phone in outrage. He was no more manageable on the phone than he was in person. What now? She could just leave. She hadn't said Tad could go with him. If he arrived and found no one home, it would serve him right. But she had food to prepare, she remembered. She exhaled in frustration. And he was right. She was too polite to leave when she knew he was coming.

With impatient movements she broke eggs into a mixing bowl, and, grabbing a whisk, took her annoyance out on the lemon soufflé. It fell.

Jesse parked his sports car in front of Betsy's house and stepped out. His eyebrows lifted in surprise. Not bad! he thought. The house was a large mock Tudor in the expensive Marina district of San Francisco. It was beautifully kept, with pots of bright flowers on the front steps, a freshly painted green door, and polished brass numerals. A discreet plaque beside the doorbell said "Calcuisine School of Food."

He stood thinking, his hands shoved characteristically into the pockets of his jeans. The wind off the bay ruffled his straight golden hair. Achieving this kind of success took a will of steel, he realized. There was more to Betsy than met the eye. The sound of laughter drifted around the side of the house, and he turned toward it in curiosity. He heard a woman's laugh, warm and slightly husky, and the wonderful, full-chested sound that children make when they're totally delighted by something.

He headed for the gate at the side of the house by instinct, following the sounds down a tiny pathway squeezed between Betsy's house and her neighbor's. The voices grew louder. "It could be lemon soup! Here, have a sip!" Betsy was being silly, and Tad could hardly speak through his laughter.

"No! No!" he hooted. Scuffling sounds suggested a chase.

"Open wide," she coaxed. "It won't hurt you, it's not gourmet." Tad couldn't speak. He was giggling helplessly.

"You're right, it's disgusting," Betsy conceded.

"F-f-foamy l-lemonade," Tad wheezed with glee.

Jesse rounded the back of the house. A wisteria-covered porch post screened him, but he could see into the kitchen through double glass doors. Betsy, dressed in jeans and a loose pink shirt under a chef's apron, held out a wooden spoon. Without her earrings, sunglasses, and reserved manner, she looked about seventeen. Jesse smiled, caught by the happy warmth of her expression. He felt a sense of triumph, like a detective stumbling over an important clue. There was *lots* more to Betsy than met the eye.

Tad, doubled over with his arms across his stomach, had tears of laughter streaming down his cheeks.

"I know," Betsy said, "we could use it for those pies they have in slapstick movie scenes, to throw at people. What a good idea!" She sounded absurdly pleased with herself. Tad, still giggling, staggered toward the bowl of runny lemon souffle and scooped up a fistful.

"Tad!" Betsy shrieked in amused alarm. "You wouldn't."

The chase reversed direction. "Here, Mom, try it, it's good," Tad insisted, gasping the words out between chuckles. "You made it yourself."

Betsy screeched as a glob of lemon foam landed squarely on her cheekbone. "You little wretch! I'll get you for that!" She grabbed a handful of the stuff and sprinted around the butcher-block island in the center of the big room. She licked at the lemon-colored blob as it ran into her smiling mouth, and cocked her arm to throw.

Jesse was grinning as broadly as the two in the kitchen, delighted by what he saw. He wanted in. If two could play, why not three?

His movement drew Betsy's gaze, and she stopped dead, her smile fading, her arm frozen in windup position.

Jesse watched the protective inner shades come down over her eyes with regret. Damn, Betsy! he pleaded silently. Don't leave. The two of them stared at each other for what seemed like minutes.

Weightless, her stomach plummeting, Betsy felt as if she were riding in an elevator when the cable had snapped. It should be illegal for a man to look as good as he did. His laughing eyes and smile-slashed cheeks knocked the air out of her lungs, and it was all she could do to keep from making a minute study of the shape his knit polo shirt revealed. And on top of that he was so blasted happy! It really wasn't fair.

"Jesse!" Tad squealed. "You're here!"

"In the flesh." He stepped into the room and held out his hand for a man-to-man handshake. He and Tad both laughed when it came away sticky.

He licked his fingers, saying teasingly to Betsy, "So you still have your failures."

"This one was your fault, actually," she replied tartly, wiping at the mess on her cheek with the back of one hand. "I decided to beat it by hand after I talked to you this morning."

"Got carried away, did you?" he grinned. "Here, hold still. I'll get that." He picked up a damp cloth and dabbed at her cheek, holding her in place with a hand on her shoulder, reminding her of how she'd done this for him just last night.

Her breath caught suddenly, surprisingly, as she was flooded with awareness of his size. He smelled clean and natural. She could feel the warmth from his body. Under his hand, her nerve endings leaped to tingling life.

"It's all right," she said jerkily, shying away from the cloth.

He watched her panic rise, keeping his hand on her shoulder. "It's done," he said slowly. "Clean and shining." Their gazes locked, hers wide and alarmed, his narrowed and interested. Whatever she claimed, he knew she wasn't indifferent to him.

Tad had rinsed his hands. "Are we really going on your ship?" he asked.

When Jesse turned to smile at the boy, Betsy moved herself out of his reach, struggling for composure. It was a casual gesture, for pity's sake! she tried to tell herself. He was wiping goo off your cheek, not caressing it. Get hold of yourself!

"It's not exactly a ship, Tad," Jesse said, "more of a boat. But yes, it's rigged and waiting. Do you think you could talk your mother into coming with us?"

Tad turned eagerly toward Betsy, who was already shaking her head. "Sorry, honey." She said it gently to soften the boy's disappointment. "I have a dinner for eight being picked up later, and no lemon soufflé. I have to do some quick improvising."

"Don't worry about feeding Tad tonight," Jesse said. "I've got a picnic packed on the boat." A teasing note entered his voice. "It's a shame you'll miss this chance to taste someone else's cooking. I fix a mean deviled egg, myself."

She smiled faintly. "I'll just get him a sweater. I won't be a minute."

Betsy practically ran down the hall. Why did he keep smiling at her? It scattered her thoughts in the strangest directions. In Tad's room, she had to remind herself what she was for.

Tad and Jesse were waiting at the front door when she returned. Jesse watched her come all the way down the stairs, thinking he knew athletes who could take pointers from her in moving fluidly. She did it totally without thought, but all her actions and gestures were made with a quiet grace. Lovely.

On the bottom step, Betsy collected another one of Jesse's smiles, this one so warm and approving that she hesitated a full second before holding the sweater out to him. He took it, still smiling.

Tad was out the door. " 'Bye, Mom."

" 'Bye, honey."

"See you later," Jesse promised.

With her arm raised in farewell and an odd feeling of abandonment in her chest, Betsy watched them walk down the front steps. Jesse had his hand on Tad's shoulder. They were deep in talk already.

Betsy folded her arms across her chest and hunched her shoulders close to her ears, feeling the chill of the marine breeze. This wasn't supposed to happen, she told herself hollowly.

• • •

The sun was setting as Betsy handed the last white box with the green-on-white Calcuisine label to Larry Ricco, a regular customer. "Cook the shellfish kabobs no longer than ten minutes," she instructed.

Larry stowed the box in the back seat of his car, then peeked into the largest container. "Ah, Betsy," he said in ecstasy, "you make pasta like an Italian. When are you going to marry me?"

She smiled down at Larry's curly head, a good six inches below hers. Larry took his food seriously. "You know I can't afford to marry you, Larry. You're my best customer. Besides, you're just trying to save on catering bills."

He smiled beatifically and rolled out a long, soulful sentence in Italian. When she quirked a questioning eyebrow, he translated, "How much are you hittin' me for this time?"

Jesse's silver sports car pulled up as she was waving good-bye to Larry. She went down the steps to collect Tad, pushing her hair back with one hand and feeling disheveled. She hoped Jesse wasn't going to start smiling at her again. She was too exhausted to summon any resistance.

Jesse got out and came around to Tad's door. His glance swept over Betsy, registering her tiredness, the food smears on her apron, and the way the colors of the sunset reflected off her skin. Pre-Raphaelite, he thought, with stained-glass. She definitely had the willowy grace and the remoteness. He felt a stir of devilishness. He wanted to break through the glass.

"Shh," he murmured, bending down to lift Tad's sleeping figure. "This is one exhausted, sunburned boy."

When she held out her arms for her son, Jesse said, "I'll carry him up. Point the way."

"I can do it, just let me. . . ."

He glinted an ironic smile at her in passing, and she suddenly found herself talking to his broad back. Darn him, he knew she didn't want to invite him inside. He was walking all over her again.

Flustered and uneasy, she followed him. "Upstairs, second on the right," she said ungraciously.

Together they undressed a groggy Tad and slid him between the sheets. Betsy would have dismissed Jesse if she'd thought it would have done any good. She noticed grudgingly that he was deft and gentle with the child.

As she kissed Tad on the cheek, he roused enough to say, "Hadda goo' time."

Jesse's voice was warm as he said softly, "Me too, Tad. 'Night."

He was leaning against the wall in the hallway, waiting, when Betsy came out of the room and closed Tad's door. He knew she'd probably love to order him off the premises.

Betsy sighed. It wasn't in her to show the door to someone who'd just been kind to her son, without making some gesture of kindness in return. "Would you like a cup of coffee?" she asked without enthusiasm.

He grinned broadly and said with exaggerated surprise, "Why, thank you." She flashed him a look that said, *You're laying it on a bit thick, fella.*

He fell into step behind her, still grinning. "Instant will be fine."

"Don't be insulting," came the answer he'd expected.

"You just can't help yourself, can you?" he teased. "Not only can't you show me the door, you can't even give me bad coffee."

"You're pressing your luck. I'm what they call 'passive-aggressive.' I can't throw you out, but you may find salt in your coffee." His chuckle echoed in the low hall. Betsy had the strange sensation of being surrounded by the warm sound.

In the kitchen, Jesse made himself at home on one of the tall stools that surrounded the ten-by-twenty-foot cooking island and looked around with interest. He'd been too absorbed in watching Betsy earlier to give the room any attention.

There was a row of ovens along one wall and a tilted mirror hung above a huge, dark restaurant stove. It was clearly a professional's kitchen, but it felt like a home too. Wooden beams and a flagstone floor gave the place character, while gleaming white walls and blue-and-white tiles gave it sparkle and freshness. Suspended from the ceiling were bunches of drying herbs, garlic and chili braids, baskets of potatoes, and onions of every color. The walls held copper molds and professional stainless steel cookware, displayed as proudly as paintings.

It was stylish and efficient. It could have appeared in *House & Garden* and possibly had, Jesse realized. This wasn't just any caterer's establishment. It was the environment of someone who was a leader in her field.

"Do you run your entire business from here?" he asked curiously.

"Not all of it, no," Betsy replied absently, concentrating on the coffee. "Just the single-affair catering and the cooking classes. We have another kitchen downtown where we prepare the food for the shops. Olivia runs that one, primarily."

Shops, he registered. She'd done well indeed. "How many shops do you have?"

"Three."

"You wouldn't want to tell me their names, would you?" he prodded gently as he watched her grinding coffee, enjoying her practiced, graceful movements.

"They're all gourmet fast foods. Calcuisine was the first," she recited obligingly. "We sell mostly fresh items there—every conceivable kind of salad, fruit tarts, that sort of thing. Then we branched out into Fasta Pasta."

She looked up in amusement as he groaned. "It was Alex's idea," she explained. "He's Olivia's son. Full of ideas. We vetoed Fastabulous."

"I should hope so."

She reached for a filter and cone. "We just opened Picnic Pickup last month. Ready-to-eat parties in a basket. It's really taken off. Olivia wants to branch out into an outlet for frozen bread doughs, but I'm not sold on that idea yet. We'd call it Doughboy."

"Another of Alex's names?"

She laughed, as she poured boiling water over the coffee grounds. "We foresee a great future for him in advertising."

She watched the coffee drip, then carried it across the room. "This'll keep you awake all night."

"That should make you feel better," he teased, drawing a reluctant chuckle from her. "Are you going to be all stiff and restrained the whole time I'm here?"

"Probably." She plunked the cup of aromatic coffee down in front of him and sat on a stool. "So there's not a lot of point in sticking around, is there?"

He ignored her comment and sniffed the coffee. "Arabica," he guessed.

She looked surprised, then suspicious. "Are you trying to impress me?"

"Any luck?" he asked cheerfully. He sipped his coffee, studying her over the rim of the cup with warm, appreciative eyes.

Something fluttered in Betsy's throat. She suddenly felt that she should have chosen a stool on the other side of the table.

Jesse set his cup down deliberately. "And now," he said, "you were going to tell me why you won't go out to dinner with me."

Her lips firmed. "And now you see why I didn't really want to give you a cup of coffee."

He smiled. "Seriously, Betsy, tell me again. I'm just a dumb jock. It takes me awhile to catch on." She gave him a smoldering look, and he grinned.

"Dumb jocks and I have nothing in common."

He considered that. "You like to cook. I like to eat."

It was her turn to grin. "In my life, that's a business transaction."

He inclined his head, acknowledging the hit. "How about, I like to cook, you like to eat?"

She raised her eyebrows consideringly. "Ah, but would I like to eat what you like to cook?"

"You'll never know if you don't try." It was a dare.

She smiled faintly. "Thanks, but I'll pass." The thought of having dinner with him was enticing enough to frighten her. Lower your guard with this man, she thought, and you'd be another crumpled tissue before you could blink.

Jesse noticed a nasty-looking cut on her thumb. Taking her hand, he held the wound to the light. Continuing his list of proposals, he said, "I'm a doctor, and you need one."

That drew a startled look from her. He gave her a wicked, sidelong glance, enjoying her surprise. "See! All dumb jocks are not alike."

She pulled her hand away, resenting the fact that she'd enjoyed his warmth and gentleness. "I'll buy a Band-Aid. It's cheaper and less complicated."

"I'm an uncomplicated doctor."

"Ha!" Then, tentatively, because she wanted to know, she asked, "Are you really a doctor?"

He nodded. "Yep. I finally qualified two years ago, after about a century of going to school in the off season. But you have to promise not to tell anyone. It's bad publicity. My fan mail drops off fifty percent if people think I'm intellectual."

He grinned wickedly at her dubious expression. "I'm not sure I believe you," she said.

"It was in the papers. Didn't you see it?"

"I don't read every word in the sports pages anymore," she said wryly.

He made a sardonic face. "Well, the columnists don't talk about it all that much. They find other aspects of my life more fascinating."

Betsy knew he was talking about the high life aspects.

"That was a bonus," he continued. "Being in school kept me out of the news."

"Not noticeably," she said ironically. He was in the society pages fairly consistently, so she still wasn't convinced that he was a doctor. "How did you manage to get your M.D.?" she asked.

"A lot of medical schools are more flexible these days,

to accommodate reentry women and aging quarterbacks, among others." His roguish dimple came and
went. "They let me space it out, six months on, six
months off. I think it helped, doing it in chunks. About
the time I got fed up with studying, I could go play
ball."

"But what about the internship?"

"That was the hard part." His expression became
serious. "School was a breeze, actually—work the mind
in the off season while the body recuperates—but the
internship was about as hard on my body as football.
No sleep for days," he said bleakly, "and I like my
sleep."

He was trying to make light of it, but she had read
the momentary grimness in his eyes. "It must have
been very difficult," she said softly.

Jesse glanced at her sympathetic face. That was the
first unguarded remark he'd had from her. He was
tempted to capitalize on it, but instead he grinned
tauntingly and said, "Finally, I've impressed you. It's
nice and all, but I wouldn't want my M.D. to sway you
too much. I admit I enjoy football better. We'll have to
look for something else in common. Maybe you need a
presentable male escort from time to time. I'm available
most week nights."

Her expression snapped back to one of irritation. He
was playing her like a fish. She shook her head. "I have
an adequate supply of male escorts, thank you, Dr.
Kincaid."

"Garrett?" he asked with a touch of scorn.

She looked surprised. "Yes, Garrett, for one."

"I said 'presentable' male escort."

"Garrett's a very charming, handsome, successful
man," she said defensively.

"I saw him, remember. And Tad says he walks like a
duck."

She bit her lip. "Well . . . maybe a little. . . ."

She caught Jesse smirking and couldn't completely
suppress her own smile. "Tad wouldn't like any boy-
friend of mine."

"He likes me," Jesse said smugly. She'd walked right into that one.

She gave him a withering look. "Yes, well, Tad's going to hear a few words tomorrow on the subject of his taste—and his mouth. Is there anything he didn't tell you?"

"Some things, I didn't ask."

She fought her amusement and lost. They smiled at each other. Betsy noted the glow that a day in the sun had given Jesse, and the hungry flare in his eyes as he looked at her. In the silence, a tension grew. She could feel heat rise in her cheeks.

"We could find lots of things in common," he said, with certainty. "That's not the problem. So tell me what is."

The problem was that she couldn't think straight around him, a voice said in Betsy's head. They probably gave training in hypnotism in his medical school.

He was waiting. Watching the laugh lines come and go around his eyes, she said slowly, "The problem is, A, you're too good-looking; B, you're a football player."

"Let's start with A. That's something I can change."

"Oh?" she drawled dubiously. "How?"

He reached for her hand and turned it palm up, studying it as if it could give him the answer. His thumb brushed idly back and forth over her wrist, sending her pulse racing.

"I could eat too much of your cooking," he suggested absently, focusing more on the texture of her skin than on his words. "Dye my hair gray." He looked up with a satisfied smile at her involuntary recoil from his last suggestion. "Any number of things. Time's on my side, here. Besides, what do you have against good-looking men, assuming their minds and senses of humor are functional?"

It was Betsy's turn to focus on her hand in his. The answer was that she'd wrecked her life once by falling for a dazzling, unreliable type, and it wasn't going to happen again. She couldn't tell Jesse that, so she murmured, "Nothing in common."

"I keep telling you, you're wrong. Here's something we have in common." His voice was slowly stroking her senses. "I'm a man. You're a woman."

Betsy felt herself being drawn to him and struggled against the feeling. "Maybe I don't really like men," she whispered.

"Maybe you don't," he agreed in a low voice. "And maybe you'll hate this, but I can't help myself." His brown eyes looked straight into her hazel ones with powerful insistence.

She sat still as he reached behind her neck to untie her apron. She could feel each beat of her heart throughout her body. Jesse's eyes looked black. His gaze flickered down to her lips, then back up to her wide eyes as he leaned closer to undo the bow at her waist. His breath feathered over her cheek, warm and moist.

Neither of them moved as the apron slithered to the floor. He cupped her head to draw her closer.

Her hands went up against his chest in a token protest, but when they smoothed rather than pushed, he brought her mouth the last inch to his, and she was lost.

It was a firm kiss, but there was no coercion in it. Only strength and a slow, melting sensuality. Jesse released a deep, audible breath in a steady, coffee-flavored stream that pulled her like undertow into a dark cavern of sensation.

She didn't hear the low moan that opened her lips and didn't consciously register the fact that his tongue was accepting the invitation and stroking the surfaces of her mouth with mind-dissolving intimacy. She only knew that when his tongue left to form the words, "Oh, Betsy," against her lips, she felt vacant. "Bettina, Betsy." The words vibrated against her lips like hungry bees.

"Hmmm," she murmured in answer, her lashes like insect wings fluttering open and closed. Wings. Bees. Butterflies and spring breezes. Memories of another day, another drugging sexual compulsion, coiled their way into her mind, bringing with them a panic that jerked her eyes open and drew her lips away from Jesse's.

"What?" He realized at once that something had snatched her back into a state of wariness.

Pulling against the steady pressure of his hand and looking at him with wide-open eyes, she said clearly, "Sex is the worst of all possible reasons for two people to get together."

He removed his hand from the back of her head. She remained staring at him in stiff defiance, and he gazed at her steadily.

"It was that bad with Brian?" he asked.

Her mouth moved with the emotions that were inside her before they burst out. "It was heaven with Brian! And then it was hell."

He waited, watching.

"You're offering me heaven," she said expressionlessly. "You'll have to excuse me. It doesn't tempt me a bit."

He said nothing, watching the color run up her face and then fade beyond paleness. She was lying, he thought. The kiss had tempted her, and that was why the walls she put up around herself had just shot up so high he'd never get over them. Not that way.

He straightened on his stool, noting the flash of surprise in her eyes. She almost overbalanced, like someone pushing when the resistance is removed, then put a toe to the floor to steady herself.

"Okay, let's leave it for now," he said mildly. "We're playing at home this week. Are you coming to the game?"

She blinked, taken aback at the abrupt change of subject. Then she shook her head slowly and emphatically. "No. I'm working. I'm usually working on the weekend. I don't have time for games." The double meaning was clear.

He nodded in quiet acceptance. "Tell Tad I'll give him a call when I can."

He got to his feet and stood looking down at her thoughtfully. She braced herself for another onslaught, either verbal or tactile. But after an endless minute he said simply, "Thanks for the coffee and conversation. Maybe we can do it again sometime, without the kissing. I'll see myself out."

He was gone before Betsy had gathered her thoughts together enough to form words. From a distance she heard the front door shut softly. She reached automatically for Jesse's cup to clear it away, and discovered that her hands were shaking. She put it down again.

"Darn the man," she whispered, echoing her own words from a week ago. Another set of words from a week ago slid into her mind. "I'd cast him as the persistent type."

It looked as though Olivia had been right. And Betsy didn't know how long she could hold out.

Four

Betsy dragged herself out of bed the next morning. Her thoughts were cloudy with a vague half-memory of a confused dream in which a football game became a stock-car race and Tad turned into Brian.

"Ohh, what a nightmare!" she muttered, smoothing tangled auburn hair off her face. She headed for the bathroom, feeling resentment toward Jesse Kincaid. He'd stirred the waters, and look what was surfacing!

Minutes later she emerged. Patting her face with a towel, she checked the clock on the bureau. Nine-thirty. Tad had been awake for hours, she thought, heading down the hall. What was he up to?

The note on his pillow was in Alex's handwriting. It read, "Dear Ms. Sleeping Beauty: Have taken Tad fishing on the wharf. We'll scrounge lunch at our house, then catch the bus to Candelero for the game. You will thus be relieved of your offspring for the entire day. For this I will expect a substantial reward. Love and all that goo, Alex. P.S. Mom will be over at ten to help you with the Barton wedding. P.P.S. Did you know you snore?"

"Beast," Betsy said fondly. Alex was a treasure. He was very protective of his mother, and since the two families had joined forces he'd appointed himself the head of both.

After she dressed she went downstairs, tied a white apron around her waist, and loaded hors d'oeuvres into catering caddies, hinged boxes with rows of slats for the serving trays. She checked on the entrees. The salmon had been poached yesterday, and the chicken breasts to be mesquite-grilled on the premises had been marinating all night.

A perky head poked around the door from the main part of the house. "Got everything all done, as usual?" Olivia's body, with rolled newspaper under one arm, followed the head.

Betsy smiled. "You know I always save you the picky stuff. You can garnish the salmon and wrap the vegetable bundles with scallions."

Olivia groaned as a matter of principle. "You're hogging the salads as usual, I suppose." She put the still rolled paper on the table.

"You think I'm letting you get your hands on my kiwis? They'd come out in rosettes or some awful thing."

This was a long-standing joke between them, but also one of the reasons for their successful collaboration. Betsy loved the flavors and textures of food and favored a simple presentation. Olivia enjoyed the finicky work that Betsy disliked. With a pastry tube in her hands, she was Botticelli.

Betsy peeled an orange, dangling a long spiral of rind. "By the way," she said, making the transition in a smooth voice, "are you Jesse Kincaid's spy in high places?"

She'd expected her friend to look guilty at the least, but Olivia wandered unconcernedly over to a refrigerator and rummaged inside. "He told me he might have some business for us," she said blithely.

Betsy stared. There was an air of suppressed glee about Olivia. "And you believed him?"

Olivia shrugged, emerging with her arms full of vegetables. "You never know. Besides," she added, kicking the door shut, "I think your love life's been on the back burner for long enough."

Betsy was indignant. "Oh, you do, do you, Mother? I had three dates last month, I'll have you know."

Olivia deposited her load and waved a dismissive hand. "Oh. Garrett."

"What does everyone have against Garrett?" Betsy demanded, hands on hips.

Olivia shrugged. "Nothing. What could anyone have against—or for—Garrett?"

"Well, it is *my* love life we're discussing? How would you like it if I set you up with Ray?" Ray, their equipment man and barbecue chef, was a love, but no one's romantic fantasy. Betsy laughed at the horrified expression on Olivia's face. "Right. That's how I felt when Jesse Kincaid showed up here."

"He was here?" Olivia asked eagerly.

Betsy pointed to a stool and said dryly, "That very spot. Would you like to kiss it?"

"I wouldn't, but maybe you would." There was no mistaking the glee now. Olivia removed the rubberband from the newspaper she'd brought, and with a flourish, placed it face up on the table.

It was the "Leisure" section, and most of it was devoted to pictures of opening night at the opera. In the center, larger than the others, was a close-up of Betsy and Jesse staring fixedly at each other. Betsy's hand held a handkerchief to Jesse's mouth, and he caressed her wrist. The caption read, "Culture is romantic for star quarterback Jesse Kincaid and his companion, food expert Bettina Carmody. No need to ask if she can cook, Jesse!"

Betsy's jaw dropped as color stained her face. Lifting her hands to her burning cheeks, she whispered, "Oh, Lord. Say it's not true."

"It's true, all right," Olivia said. "Do you want to tell me more about how cold Jesse Kincaid leaves you?"

"Can I tell you when I get back? I'm thinking about skipping town for a week or so."

Olivia chuckled and patted her on the back. "It'll be good for business. Do you have any idea how many women would pay to be seen with Jesse Kincaid?"

Betsy's mouth twisted wryly. She straightened and heaved a resigned sigh. "I know of one, at least. He should charge for his services."

They were ready and the truck was loaded for the wedding in plenty of time. Betsy watched Olivia climb into the cab of the truck beside Ray. "You're sure you can manage? I'll come if you think you'll need me."

Two heads shook. "They're supplying the waiters," Olivia said. "All we have to do is arrange the buffet, heat hors d'oeuvres, and grill the chicken. Besides, we lose your value as a glamorous figurehead if you're seen slaving over a hot fire."

Betsy smiled faintly, but she knew Olivia was right. This house, her own wardrobe, the imported tile and custom-designed packaging were all legitimate business expenses. They provided publicity and the ambiance that was so much a part of success in the food business these days. Style was everything, and Betsy set the style of Calcuisine.

"Okay," she conceded. "I'll work out the details of my demonstration for tomorrow's *San Francisco Today* program."

"Knock 'em dead, Betsy," Ray commanded. "You're a natural for TV."

"What are you going to wear?" Olivia asked.

Betsy nibbled on her thumb. "An apron?"

That wasn't worthy of comment. "Wear a solid color," Olivia dictated. "A pattern would detract from the patterns of the food. If the food's dark, wear something light, and vice versa. Small earrings, no bracelets. But not too plain. Choose something with striking lines."

Betsy nodded. Olivia had an instinct for these things, part and parcel of her talent for drama and presentation. "All right. See you later, you two. Don't forget to get the check."

As the truck pulled away from the alley behind Betsy's garden, Olivia fired a parting shot. "Enjoy the game!"

Betsy's lips pursed and her eyes flashed. Now how did Olivia know she was toying with the idea of tuning in the game?

She wouldn't, she decided. Olivia was wrong about her attraction to Jesse Kincaid, and she was strong-minded enough to prove it to her!

It was third down and long yardage for the Miners, an obvious passing situation. Betsy glared at the TV, which was mounted on the wall in her kitchen, not sure if she was angry at what was happening on the screen or at herself for watching it. The ingredients for tulip cookies and banana sorbet lay untouched on the table in front of her.

"Be careful, Kincaid," she murmured. "If you're going to get killed, do it when I'm not looking."

The ball was snapped and Jesse stepped back to pass. All his receivers were covered. Two linebackers bore down on him, one from each side. He danced, feinted, and dodged forward, letting their momentum take them yards behind him. He searched the field.

"Kincaid's looking toward the end zone," the announcer droned. *"He fires,"* the man's voice became animated. *"It's long to Tanner, Tanner reaches for it, bobbles it. He caught it in the end zone! Touchdown, Miners! Was that a pass? Was that a catch? That's one for the record books."* The announcer was almost incoherent with excitement.

Betsy sagged in relief. "Hooray," she mumbled weakly.

The crowd shouted as one, "Ki-i-in-cai-ai-aid!" in what had become a tradition with Miners' fans on passing touchdowns. The microphones picked up the exulting sound clearly.

Watching the screen, Betsy saw Jesse and Hap Tanner come off the field with their arms around each other, murmuring helmet to helmet, like unlikely lovers. The extra point kick was good and she continued to stare at the television, waiting for the close-up that usually followed spectacular play.

The camera closed in. From the side, she could see Jesse, helmetless now, with his hair sweat-streaked and awry, sharing his jubilation with teammates on the bench. He rubbed his face and neck with a towel and accepted the drink held out by a trainer. When he became aware of the cameraman, he turned toward him. Pointing an index finger straight at the camera, he mouthed, "Hi, Betsy."

At first Betsy assumed he'd said, "Hi, Mom," as most players did. But when he winked, the shape of his mouth registered. He'd said, "Hi, Betsy!"

Hot color ran up her neck. She gasped and jumped to her feet.

"Dammit!" she said. "Can't I have any privacy in my own home? And why won't anyone believe I'm not interested in that man?"

By the time the game was over, Betsy was limp from the strain of worrying about Jesse getting hurt and from fighting her attraction to him. And still she couldn't make herself turn the TV off.

The cameras followed the victorious Miners into the locker room and hovered around Jesse, the hero of the hour. His center, Andy White, was saying, "Boy, didn't I make him look good out there today?"

"You!" Jesse argued. "If I didn't know how to run, I'd be a pancake!"

He grinned and Betsy's glare deepened. Why did he have to smile like that, with his eyes laughing and his dimples flashing? And why couldn't he leave his uniform on until after the interviews? He looked too human in a sweat-patched T-shirt that showed the muscular length of his arms.

The interviewer was saying, "Well, Jesse, you had a terrific game. Congratulations. Did you feel better than usual out there today, or were the breaks just going your way?"

"Thanks, Stan," Jesse said. "Luck's always a big factor in a game." Betsy gave his image a jaundiced scowl.

Cut the manly modesty, Kincaid, she thought. We know all about your ego.

"But today I had an added incentive," he went on. "Someone special was watching." Betsy gasped. If he dared mention her again . . . !

He reached out a long arm to draw a small body into camera range.

"Tad!" It came out a strangled squeak. Her son beamed at the camera like an ad for lightbulbs. Jesse had his hand on Tad's shoulder and was smiling down at him.

"This young man asked me to throw a couple of long ones," he explained. "How could I refuse?"

The interviewer laughed. "Well, young man, are you satisfied?"

Tad looked up at Jesse in adoration and breathed, "You bet."

A shaft of pain lanced through Betsy's chest. Her eyes closed and she bit her lip so hard it hurt. Oh, Tad! she thought in anguish. He should have a dad. That should be Brian there with a hand on his shoulder, making him feel big and proud.

But she couldn't see Brian doing what Jesse Kincaid had just done. Brian would never have taken the time to make a lonely boy feel special, or shared the limelight with him.

Tears slid out beneath Betsy's closed eyelids. She didn't hear the interviewer move on to other players and coaches. She noted in amazement that she was crying.

Tad needs a father, she thought. *And I'm lonely.*

It was an admission she hadn't made in all the years of struggle she'd faced since Brian's death. On its heels came the question, why was she fighting so hard to keep Jesse Kincaid out of her life? He was becoming a fixture in her mind.

She raised her head to consider. Reaching for a tissue, she blew her nose.

It was because of what he was, she tried to tell herself. Flashy, arrogant, pushy, with too much surface charm and physical appeal to know anything about fidelity. He wasn't her kind of man.

An ingrained honesty pulled her up short. Oh, all right. So she was human, and female. He appealed to her, she admitted it. And, okay, maybe he did have brains and kindness and a sense of humor too.

She wandered over to the French doors to stare out at the light drizzle of rain glossing the trees in the garden. She folded her arms across her chest and huddled into them. Allowing herself to like Jesse made her feel vulnerable.

She resisted him because he brought up so much that was still too raw, she whispered to herself. He aroused in her many of the emotions that had nearly wrecked her life.

It wasn't enough that he made her heart go pitter-patter. She'd come a long way, but she had a long, long way to go before she was strong enough to survive a love affair with the likes of Jesse Kincaid.

Tad nagged and cajoled Betsy out of bed at six the next morning. "Please, Mom. C'mon. We'll have time to fly the kite if you just get up. You promised we'd do it this week. C'mon, Mom. I'm all ready for school, see?"

He practically dressed her, fetching socks, tennis shoes, and windbreaker, ignoring her grumbles.

"This will not be fun, Tad," she muttered. "Zombies are not good company. I need a cup of coffee. Aren't you hungry?"

"C'mon, Mom, you'll love it. You don't have to comb your hair, just wear your hood."

On that she stood firm. "I'm not going out of the house without washing my face, brushing my teeth, and combing my hair, so just sit down and twiddle your thumbs for a bit, darling."

Once out on the Marina Green, with the cool, moist breeze from the bay chasing the cobwebs from her mind and the sun slicing through patchy fog, Betsy began to enjoy herself.

"You're right, it's nice out here, Tadpole, but I hate to tell you—no wind."

Tad shrugged philosophically and reached into his jacket. "That's okay, I brought a football too."

Betsy closed one eye and regarded the light of her life suspiciously. She'd been wondering what he was hiding. "I smell a plot." She watched him grin cheerfully and stow the kite under a bench. "You didn't even bring the string."

He was waving her back. "Farther, Mom, farther. I want to practice punting."

She backed up, talking to herself. "Punting, okay. Punting I can handle. Kickers live to old age." Then she shouted, "Far enough?"

"That's good. Ready?" The first drop kick he missed completely. He lost his balance and fell on top of the ball.

Betsy cupped her hands around her mouth and yelled, "We'll call it a blocked kick." Tad got up laughing, and tried again, with more success.

Betsy was puffing by the time he'd tired of kicking and inevitably moved on to passing. She caught a high, wobbly one, thinking maybe she should hire a male, football-playing babysitter for Tad in the afternoons, and called, "When do I get to throw and you catch?"

"One more, Mom. Run for it!"

It was sailing over her head. She considered letting it go, then thought, Come on, you're all he's got, and took off at a run, hands outstretched, head turned back to follow the flight of the ball.

She wasn't going to get it. As it passed by her, a flash of pale blue cloth and tanned skin snagged the ball out of the air and came down in front of her. Collision was unavoidable.

"Oof!" The body in front of her was falling backward, so the impact wasn't too great, but momentum took them both down together.

She landed in a tangle of limbs, rolled once, then raised herself off the blue T-shirt and focused on the face—Jesse Kincaid's face—grinning up at her.

"Interception," he said.

"You!" she exclaimed, all the breath driven out of her lungs. "What are you doing here?"

She levered herself off him and struggled to her knees, where she remained, staring from his innocent grin to Tad's gleeful face as the boy trotted toward them.

"Just passing by," Jesse claimed, rising to a sitting position and tossing the ball idly.

"Jesse! You made it!" Tad called out, making a liar of his hero.

"Hi, Squirt," Jesse called, and smiled cheerfully at Betsy's glowering face. "I do run down here from time to time," he added apologetically.

It was feasible, she thought. There were runners all around them, but still she suspected a conspiracy. He and Tad had set this up yesterday in the locker room, she guessed.

She should have been angry—he was paying no attention to the fact that she didn't want to be involved with him—but he looked very good, the healthy tan of his muscular arms and legs set off by sky-blue running clothes.

Little laugh lines appeared at the corners of his eyes in response to the reluctant smile twitching at her lips. It wasn't complete capitulation, though.

"You and I need to have a little talk," she said warningly.

"Any time," came the too-swift reply.

"About the dangers of undermining parental authority in the American family."

"What parental authority? Tad runs your family, that's clear."

She glared at him indignantly. "If you're trying to be charming, you have a long way to go."

His eyes widened in mock innocence. "I thought all I had to do was be impressive on the football field." He chuckled at her withering look and turned to Tad, who was saying enthusiastically, "Now we can have a real game!"

"Jesse's just running by, Tad," Betsy said ironically.

Tad glanced anxiously at Jesse. "He'll play, won't you, Jesse?" Jesse rose fluidly to his feet and held a hand out to Betsy. His dark eyes sent private messages. "I'll take football over running any day. Who wants to be quarterback?"

"It's Mom's turn, really," Tad said fairly.

Betsy groaned. "Can't I be referee?"

"Tad, why don't you be quarterback? Your mom's got real potential as a wide receiver, but she needs practice." He winked at Betsy.

"You, I suppose," she said with resignation, "are going to be cornerback again?"

He leered at her. "Do you know a better way to get your hands on the . . . uh, ball?"

She laughed aloud. She couldn't help herself. It was a crisp, fresh morning, Tad's little face was completely happy, and Jesse, say what she might about him, was stimulating company.

Maybe it was the sense of danger he carried with him, but he made her feel alive. He made the wind sharper, and the grass springier under her feet.

It was even a tiny bit exhilarating, she admitted to herself, to be pursued by an attractive man. She'd keep running, because she had a well-developed sense of self-preservation, but it couldn't hurt, could it, to give in this once to the excitement Jesse Kincaid created in her? Tad was here, and it was a public place. What could happen?

Later they walked home, with Tad between them hanging onto both their hands. They'd had a good time together. Jesse had been charming and funny, showing off, teasing Tad. Once he'd lifted the laughing boy bodily and carried him like a football to the "end zone," pretending surprise at finding that it was Tad he had under his arm and not the ball.

They were all tousled and grubby and so totally at ease with each other that when Jesse said, "That was fun. Can I take you two to dinner tonight?" Betsy almost answered, "Sure, why not?"

With her mouth open to say the words, she looked

sharply over at him. How had he lulled her into a false sense of security so easily? What could happen on Marina Green? she'd asked herself earlier. Well, what could happen was that she could become so addicted to Jesse Kincaid's dangerous charm that she'd find herself on his heap of discarded women before nightfall.

She pictured the look of sick anger on the face of the brunette at the opera house. The woman had been angry because of Jesse's callous indifference. Never forget it, she told herself. He might be attractive, but Mr. Nice Guy he was not. He was an unscrupulous man who'd use a child to complete a conquest if he needed to. He was using Tad. Heaven knew why, but he was after her at the moment, and he was a master of the chase.

Her mouth snapped shut in a "No." When Jesse and Tad both looked surprised at her vehemence, she softened it. "I'm sorry, but tonight's schedule is full. Thanks anyway, Jesse."

"Maybe some other time," he murmured, looking thoughtful.

"Aww, Mom, why not? Please, can't we go?"

Gently but firmly Betsy said, "I have other plans, Tad. Don't nag, now. You've had a special outing this morning. Let that be enough for today."

The boy's enthusiasm subsided, and he thrust out his lower lip and kicked at the sidewalk. Then he looked up with a quick gleam of hope. "Well, at least you can stay for breakfast, Jesse, right, Mom?"

What could she say? "Sure, if he likes corn flakes," she said dryly. "That's all we have time for."

"I love 'em." Jesse looked at her searchingly, but she avoided his eyes. "Do you think you could drop me off at my place after you take Tad to school, Betsy? I'll be late for practice if I have to run home."

She doubted that, but again Tad answered for her. "Sure she could, right, Mom? She has to get out the car to take me, anyway."

Betsy mounted the front steps and inserted the key in the lock. "My pleasure," she muttered.

They dropped Tad off at school just as the bell was ringing. He scrambled from the car and dashed into the building, calling out good-byes.

"Drat," said Betsy, reaching for the lunchbox on the floor of the car, "he's forgotten his lunch."

"I'll take it. Where's his classroom?"

"No!" she said emphatically. "The class would be in an uproar all day if you appeared. Even first and second graders know who you are. I'll just be a minute."

Jesse sank back against the seat and watched Betsy's slim form run gracefully across the empty schoolyard. His mouth twisted. It wasn't always an advantage to be Jesse Kincaid. He'd probably have a better chance with Betsy if he drove a cablecar.

They were quiet during the ride to his North Beach house. He sat sideways to study Betsy. Her rich hair was still tousled and she wore no makeup at all. With her clear eyes and creamy skin, she looked as fresh as the morning. The peach shade of her windbreaker brought out delicate color in her cheeks. He wondered how she could be as beautiful fresh from bed in the morning as she was in satin and velvet in the evening. Her glow came from the inside, he decided.

Betsy felt her muscles tightening. She cleared her throat. "Do I have milk on my mouth?" she asked in a husky voice.

He flashed her a grin and leaned closer, pretending to search. "Nope," he admitted, "I was just admiring you."

She swallowed and said in gentle protest, "Jesse."

"I know, I'm embarrassing you." He continued to stare.

The color under her smooth skin deepened. It wasn't just his staring that was getting to her. She was too aware of his strong, hair-crisped brown legs near hers and his arm, which lay along the back of the seat, touching her shoulder. Paradoxical thoughts chased themselves through her head. She wished she'd paid more attention to her hair and clothes this morning, and she wished he'd stop looking at her. She could have squirmed with discomfort.

"Which way now?"

"Top of the hill and turn right. Then make a U. It's the second building." She turned into a cul-de-sac and pulled up to where he pointed.

"Is this it?" she asked, peering across Jesse at the modern, wood-shingled building.

The relief in her voice made him grin. "Yeah, but you can come in if you're not ready to let me go."

"You must have a good view from here."

"Come in and see?" he asked.

She shook her head. "You'll be late for work."

He regarded her curiously, making no move to leave the car. "Tell me something. Back there on the green, when I asked you and Tad out to dinner, I had the impression you almost said yes. Was I right?"

She looked at him sideways, both hands still gripping the wheel, and answered indirectly. "It was a bit unfair, don't you think, to use Tad as leverage? You knew he'd be disappointed if I said no."

Jesse looked startled, then thoughtful. He nodded gravely and said, "I didn't mean it like that—I just wanted to be with both of you—but I see your point. From now on, I'll pass out separate invitations, and I'll check my plans for Tad with you first."

That wasn't quite what she had in mind. She wanted him to leave them both alone, but she said nothing. He glanced at her, reading her silence. "Is it all right if I take him for a hamburger one night this week? Since I have mentioned it?" She nodded reluctantly, knowing Tad would be upset if he didn't hear from Jesse.

With a challenging gleam in his eye, Jesse said, "Now, about you and me."

Her breathing became constricted. "I don't see a you and me, Jesse."

"I do," he said softly, "very clearly." He lifted his hand from the back of the seat to touch her cheek in a feather soft caress. Longing shot through her, and she closed her eyes momentarily.

Inside she was begging him, *please don't press it, Jesse.* He could have it all, so easily, and she'd end up in little pieces. The price for a fling with him would be more than she could afford.

His eyes never leaving her face, he said, "I have a feeling that the way you feel about me says yes, Betsy. It's some idea in your head that's saying no." He paused for an answer. When none came he added, "I hate most reporters, you know, and I haven't exactly been slow to say so. That's one reason they hound me, and that's one reason for my public image. You're not buying the popular picture of me, are you?"

Was she? Betsy asked herself. Well, maybe, but she had some personal corroboration. She knew he made remarks in the locker room about other men's wives, and she knew he could drop a lover without a backward glance when he saw someone else he wanted. She'd seen him in brawls on the football field, and she'd seen him attack a photographer just three nights ago. "Maybe I'm buying the unpopular one." She smiled unexpectedly.

He smiled, too, slowly and seductively. "You could at least give me a chance to tell my side of the story. Besides, we were going to have a talk about outside interference in parenting."

Betsy's pulse rate was sending her a message that danger was near. Breathlessly she said, "I'll mail you a child psychology book."

He leaned toward her and took a lock of her hair in his fingers. "We'll trade. I'll send you one on human sexuality."

Heat rushed into her cheeks. She jerked her head aside and whispered between clenched teeth, "Jesse! You are so outrageous."

He felt a deep satisfaction at her reaction, and tugged on her hair. She turned toward him. He continued the pressure, smiling warmly. He wanted her to come to him.

Betsy couldn't believe how strong the temptation was. Her chest heaved and her lips parted in a helpless sigh.

His eyes darted down to her mouth, his smile fading. The air in the car felt thick with the tension between them.

He dropped her hair and slid his hand behind her neck. With gentle pressure he brought her lips to his. His eyes burned into hers as he moved his head slowly from side to side, stroking her lips with his.

She was melting. She seemed to have no will of her own. "Oh, drat," she whispered as her eyes closed.

Against her lips he murmured, "I can't stop thinking about you. I can't stay away from you. Touch me, Betsy."

Her hands lifted to rest on his shoulders, which were warm under the thin knit shirt he wore. He moaned and slid urgent fingers into her hair to bring her even closer. She leaned against him, her head dropping back under his kiss. How could he do this to her? How could she let this happen? she wondered before thinking hazed into sensation.

His hand clenched in her hair. *Whoa, Jess,* he told himself. *Don't frighten her.* Only with her did he come so close to losing control, so fast, he realized. Her nearness flooded him with fervent wanting.

Betsy moaned softly under the fierce pressure of his lips. She was slipping, slipping . . . She didn't hear his front door opening. But Jesse heard it. With his hand still buried in Betsy's hair, he turned toward the sound.

At the open door to his house stood a woman shaking a dust mop. Betsy felt shock stiffen his body before she pulled away from him, humiliation crawling through her.

It wasn't the opera-house brunette. This woman was blond and buxom, with luxuriant, Nashville-style curls and tight jeans. She had a bold, taunting expression on her face.

Betsy dragged in breath and drew her defenses around her. "The housekeeper?" she asked with brittle sarcasm.

Jesse heard her voice shake under her sarcasm. He whipped toward her with a despairing look before turning back to the blond. "Rita! What are you doing here?"

he demanded. He opened the car and stood half in and half out, glaring at Rita.

"We-yal, I just used ma little ol' key, Jesse dawlin'," came the reply in a heavy Texas accent. "And you know ah can't sta-yund mess."

Jesse closed his eyes and hit his forehead with the palm of his hand. Turning to Betsy he said fast and low, "I haven't seen her in months, Betsy."

"Do tell," she drawled, feigning indifference. "If you'll just get out, Jesse, I'll be on my way. You and Rita can talk over old times."

"Betsy!" he spat. "For God's sake give me a chance. Rita and I were finished months ago!" Pivoting swiftly toward the blond, who was watching the scene with amused interest, he said between his teeth, "Tell her, Rita."

Rita was a study in confused innocence. "Tell her what, dawlin'?"

"Dammit!" He turned to Betsy and just stared in blank frustration, willing her to believe him.

She gazed back at him, wanting to laugh and cry. The funny thing was, she did believe him. She thought he probably hadn't seen Rita in a while and he wasn't all that involved with the glamorous brunette. And it changed nothing. What was she doing here with a man who lived a soap-opera life? Why was she letting herself be part of these absurd scenes?

In a voice that held an edge of hysterical laughter she said, "Doesn't it get complicated, balancing all these exes? Jesse, please shut the car door. I have to go."

His clenched fist came down to pound the dashboard, but just before impact he controlled it to make only a small thump. "Listen to me!" he said between clenched teeth. "None of this"—he waved a hand to indicate the drama taking place at his front door—"has anything to do with me."

She did laugh at that.

He was scowling in earnestness. "I'm not having much luck showing you, so I'm telling you." He gave each word heavy emphasis. "I am a nice person."

She raised her brows. "*Everyone* seems to think so."

He remained staring at her and she began to feel desperate. "For Pete's sake, go away, Jesse! I want to get out of here!"

With a final glare of frustration he heaved himself upright and closed the door harder than was necessary.

Betsy quickly put the car in gear and pulled away. In the rear-view mirror she saw Jesse turn toward Rita with controlled fury visible in every line of his body. She doubted if Rita would find him a nice person.

Good luck, Rita, she thought, and thanks.

She blew out an unsteady breath. She'd remember Rita. Rita had saved her from making a very big fool of herself.

But how many more times could she count on help of that kind from the Ritas of the world? she asked herself. She'd known all along what style of life Jesse Kincaid led, and still she turned to jelly when he got close to her.

There wouldn't be any more saviors, and she couldn't depend on her own common sense. She'd just have to make sure she stayed far away from Jesse Kincaid.

Five

When the phone rang one day the following week, Betsy snatched it off the hook hoping it was Olivia. She'd left a hasty message on the answering machine in the downtown kitchen.

"Hello?" she said urgently.

"What's cooking?" Jesse asked in a deep, relaxed tone of voice.

Betsy's shoulders sagged. She was too preoccupied to worry about their last meeting. "Me," she blurted. "Simmering. The garbage collectors took three bags of freshly washed lettuce along with the trash." He chuckled.

"It's not funny! I have a class in an hour, and I need that lettuce! I thought you were Olivia."

"I have to be Olivia for you to be glad to hear from me?" he teased.

"Jesse," she said in a goaded tone. "I don't have time for romantic repartee just now."

"Well, actually this was a business call. But I don't know if you're the firm for us. You don't sound all that businesslike today." His amusement was clearly evident in his voice.

"What are you talking about?" She resigned herself to being patient.

"I need a caterer. Or actually, we do. The team. I . . .

uh, mentioned your name to the right person." His voice dripped smugness, and Betsy had to laugh.

"Message received," she said. " 'Jesse Kincaid is not only a nice guy but also a valuable business contact.' "

"That's it, but you should add, 'and I owe him a favor.' "

Had she really expected him to be apologetic after the episode with Rita? Insolence was more in character for him. "Since you're totally unscrupulous and not above taking advantage, I'll just say, Thanks, but no thanks."

"You misjudge me!" he said in a wounded tone. "A joke's a joke, but this is a bona fide business proposition."

She bit her lip. She couldn't afford to turn down a big party just now. "What did you have in mind?"

"Nothing terribly challenging. It's an outdoor picnic, the annual big event for families and all."

"What kind of food did you want?"

"Hamburgers?" he asked apologetically.

"Hamburgers!" she said in revolted tones, making him laugh.

"Hamburgers," he stipulated firmly. "No sauces."

"No sauces?" she repeated wistfully.

"No sauces."

"It costs extra for me to do violence to my principles."

He laughed. "No problem. Make us pay through the nose."

"I'm going to have to think about it. Can you give me a date, approximate number of people, and price range?"

"I take it back, you are businesslike. Can't we get together to discuss it?"

"Are you the person in charge?" she asked, knowing the answer.

"You have a low, suspicious mind."

She smiled. "Also accurate."

His voice took on warmer overtones. "Betsy, will you go out to dinner with me this week?"

"No." Her answer was as firm as before, but less abrupt.

"A movie?"

"No, but thanks, Jesse."

"A walk around the block?"

She laughed in answer.

"You're not going to hold last week's fiasco against me, are you, Betsy?"

"Of course not!" she said falsely.

"Good. I knew you were too fair to make me pay for a set-up."

"Absolutely!"

"So you will go out with me?"

"Nope."

There was a silence. Then Jesse said with some surprise, "You know, you're tough. You say things quietly, but you stick like glue."

"I couldn't have built a business and a life for my son if I didn't."

With droll regret he protested, "Oh, Betsy, I wish you didn't class getting rid of me with your life's highest imperatives. Is it really that urgent?" His tone invited her to smile.

"I think I like you least when you force me to laugh."

"I know. A sense of humor's a real liability sometimes. Let's talk about it."

"No."

"Could you try that in a shriek? Maybe I'm thick, but I just have trouble believing you mean it when you say it so sweetly."

"Believe it."

A doubting "hmmm" came over the line.

"I mean it." She hoped he couldn't tell she was grinning.

"Better," he said dubiously, "but not great."

Laughing, but exasperated, she said, "Jesse!"

He chuckled. "There, you got it. Okay, I'm gone."

There was a click, then a hum as he hung up on her. She took a deep breath and stared at the phone. What was she going to do about him? Staying away from him might not be good enough. Even on the phone, he was dangerously appealing.

• • •

Olivia was thrilled at the prospect of catering the Miners' picnic. "Of course we'll do it! It'll be fun, besides being terrific publicity. We could drop a hint to that reporter in the 'Bay City Living' section. He could just come by for some pictures—"

"They could just politely throw us out on our ear," Betsy concluded. "The Miners control their public relations very carefully. The most we can hope for is a mention in 'Eating-Around-the-Bay.' "

"You're probably right," Olivia said regretfully. Then, stiffening, she remembered her due. "While we're on the subject, don't you owe me an apology?"

"Do I?" Betsy asked mildly.

"I told you Jesse had a business proposition for you."

"With the emphasis on 'proposition,' " Betsy said dryly. "But I'll apologize if you like. Forgive me, darling Olivia. You can send me as many men on the make as you like if it results in business."

Olivia tried to convince Betsy she'd be needed at the picnic, but Betsy didn't buy it. "You and Jesse think alike, but I've endured enough Miner social affairs. Never again. If you need another person, take Alex."

Olivia looked at her curiously, but Betsy didn't elaborate. It was bad enough remembering those occasions— her wearing a stiff, false smile, Brian in the corner laughing with his cronies, probably about her, and real or imagined pity on the faces around her. She wasn't eager to talk about it, but the idea of attending that picnic generated real panic.

In the end, Olivia took Alex, Ray, and Tad, whose clamoring had worn Betsy down. Betsy watched them leave, with a worried look in her eyes. Alex had been cutting up all day, and Tad was seriously overexcited. She hoped they would behave themselves.

She wasn't altogether surprised when Jesse called a

couple of hours later. "Betsy, I think you'd better get on down here." His voice was grave and clipped.

"Why?" she asked weakly.

"I'm not sure you'd like what's going on."

She was at the Miners' practice fields half an hour later. Jesse met her at the entrance. "Glad you could make it," he said. His finger lifted to the tip of her eyebrow, then drifted in a light caress to the corner of her mouth.

The touch shocked her. She gazed at him, eyes wide and heart hammering, forgetting for the moment what she was doing there. A little frisson of fear traveled down her spine. That was all it took—a feather touch on her cheek—to narrow her world to him. She didn't know how he did it, but it scared her to death. She didn't want anyone to have that kind of power over her.

Not until his lips curved slowly did her gaze sharpen to wariness. "What's the trouble?" she asked, jerking her gaze from his and surveying the field before her.

Music played on the loudspeakers. She heard children's voices calling, and snatches of laughter.

"Over there," Jesse said, nodding toward the crowd bunched around the food stations. As he guided her through clumps of people who were eating and talking, she heard scattered snippets of football shop talk.

"He's thinking Pro Bowl. Has a chance, too, with McDowell out for the season."

"Mine's unbearable for two full days before a game. Afterwards, he's not so bad. He's too tired to make trouble. I tell you, I live for the off season."

"What's the point of all these contact drills? We've got enough injuries already."

"We'll be lucky if he can fit a few games in between endorsements."

Feeling like she'd entered a time warp, or a nightmare, Betsy had to drag her mind back to business.

She searched the field and spotted Olivia talking and laughing with a couple of Miners while keeping a sharp eye on things. People were moving past the buffet in good order. The food looked great: three kinds of potato salad; cole slaw; tomato, mozzarella, and basil salad; orange-jicama salad; guacamole; and, of course, deviled eggs. For dessert there was chocolate cake, coconut cake, apple-almond cake, homemade ice-cream, and a watermelon that Olivia had carved into a swan and filled with melon balls. Betsy had stayed within their specifications, but this would be a picnic the Miners would never forget.

Ray was serving lemonade to a bunch of kids while the adults helped themselves to beer and iced tea from nearby spigots. He caught her eye and winked.

Alex was on duty, even if he was flipping the burgers higher than necessary to impress a couple of teenaged admirers. At one end of the big field Tad played football with a group of kids, but she really hadn't expected him to be any help.

"What?" she asked in confusion. "It seems okay to me."

Jesse waved an inclusive hand at her employees. "Well, look at them. They're having a wonderful time. Isn't that rather unprofessional?"

She glanced at his deadpan face and said dangerously, "Jesse, you unscrupulous, manipulative . . ." Words failed her.

He smiled down at her, his eyes warm. It was the smile that haunted her dreams, but for once she was too upset to respond.

"I'm not staying," she snapped.

"You're going to disappoint a lot of folks, then." He indicated a petite redhead who was making her way toward them. "In fact, that's one reason I called you. No one could believe you'd cater this affair and not show up yourself to say hello to old friends. I'm saving your reputation."

"I could kill you for this. Look at me." She indicated her comfortable jeans and sweater.

He looked at her and said, "Very nice." When her glare grew in malevolence, he added, "It's a picnic, not a PR session. Smile, if you're concerned about your image."

Jesse knew what he was up against. Betsy hated being here. Life with Brian had been hell, she'd said, and all these people were part of that life. Of course she didn't want anything to do with them.

But he wanted something to do with her, he thought, looking at her glorious, furious face. He wanted a lot to do with her, and if he had to drag her here by the hair to show her he wasn't Brian, so be it.

Betsy seesawed between anger and despair. Being with Jesse was a danger to her at the best of times, but doing it here, among all the ghosts of past humiliations, was adding unbearable tension to the usual turmoil he created in her. He couldn't know what he was doing to her.

"Later," she said through stiff lips. "I'm going to kill you later."

"It's a date. Finally." He made no effort to disguise the triumph or the taunt. With Jesse's words ringing in her ears, Betsy turned to Molly Collins.

"Betsy!" Molly shouted eagerly. She reached out both hands for Betsy's. "I'm so glad to find you again. I called and called three years ago, but you just dropped out of sight." Molly's green eyes blazed from a face sprinkled with freckles.

"Molly, it's good to see you," Betsy said, surprised to find that she meant it. She'd always liked Molly, and Molly had seemed to like her. Betsy hadn't given her much encouragement. In those days, every friendly gesture had seemed like charity. "How have you been?"

"Pregnant, mostly," Molly said with a gurgle of laughter. "I have two more children. I've forgotten how to cook anything but peanut-butter sandwiches. Can I come to one of your classes?"

"I have a few spaces left in next week's session."

"I'll be there! Uh-oh, Eric's going to knock that table down, gotta run!" She literally did, and scooped up a toddler with his hands full of tablecloth.

After Molly, there were more old acquaintances to greet. Jesse kept a hand on Betsy's elbow and moved her from one to the other as if they were passing down a receiving line. When they came to a group of Brian's old cronies, he lingered, ignoring Betsy's stiff resistance.

"Will," he said. "Jay, Morton. You all remember Bettina Carmody, don't you?"

Betsy could hardly see through her haze of anger and humiliation, but she was aware that all three men had bobbed uneasy, sheepish heads. Jesse waited for the silence to get uncomfortable. Finally, Will Fanning said, "Mrs. Carmody. How've you been?"

"Fine. Widowhood definitely has its points." Betsy couldn't believe that flippant, brittle voice was hers, but Brian's buddies all laughed in surprise, and Will looked at her with new respect.

Jesse smiled at her and moved her along. "There's Tad. Let's tell him you're here. See you three later."

The three men nodded their heads. "Mrs. Carmody, a pleasure."

Betsy said good-bye and let Jesse lead her off. "You've got a real talent for manipulating people," she murmured, looking straight ahead.

He didn't look at her either, but his lips twitched. "It's called leadership ability. Crucial quality for a quarterback."

"I don't want to be here." It was almost a plea, and this time she did look upward through her eyelashes.

He glanced down at her with understanding. "I know, you don't like football players. We're all a bunch of dumb jocks."

She released a short breath of irritation. "You make me sound like a narrow-minded bigot." She ignored his wide-eyed expression of agreement. "I just like to choose my own friends these days."

"There are a lot of people to choose from. Some of Brian's friends were dumb jocks. Mine are not. I'd like you to meet some of them." He said it gently, but he wasn't going to back down.

Betsy sighed. Even with Jesse's breadth behind and

above her like a bulwark during these unwelcome encounters she felt like a stretched spring. She glanced longingly toward the parking lot. What would he do, she wondered, if she just said, "Well, it's been nice seeing everyone, but I've got to go now"?

His hand tightened on her shoulder as he murmured, "Don't even consider it." The look she gave him was one of dislike. He was a truant officer, not a bulwark.

He smiled. In his present mood, he was probably capable of putting her in a hammerlock to keep her there. Her chin jutted out. "I think I'll check on the food." With a slicing look at Jesse, she added, "That is why I'm here." He nodded agreeably and fell into step.

"Don't let me keep you, Jesse," she said sweetly.

"You're not," he said blandly. "This is exactly where I want to be."

"But surely you have other people to bully?"

He looked down at her, enjoying the sparks. "Nobody important."

As they neared the grills, a junior version of Jesse's taunting smile spread across Alex's face. "Betsy, you came! Couldn't keep away, huh?" His eyes flashed meaningfully to Jesse and back to her.

She looked him straight in the eye. "Finish that thought and you're fired," she said levelly. Alex contented himself with a laugh.

She nodded at the burgers on the grill. "Those look good."

"Want one?" Before she could refuse, Jesse said, "She'd love one. It'll do wonders for her disposition."

Glowering at Jesse, she said, "Meet Big Brother, Alex. If you ever need someone to run your life, give him a call."

Alex grinned sympathetically at Jesse and handed him the hamburger. Jesse in turn held it out to her, but she walked past him. "Eat it yourself," she said. "You ordered it."

He followed her, taking a bite of the burger. "How long are you going to sulk?" he asked.

"I'm not sulking." Then, more or less admitting she was, she said again, "I don't want to be here."

"Why don't you just slug me? Get it out of your system, then we can have a good time."

"I refuse to have a good time. That would be sanctioning fraud and misrepresentation." He laughed, and she had to prim her lips to keep from joining in.

"Ah, Betsy, it's punishment enough being near you and not being able to touch you. Have a heart."

As a quick thrill shot through her, she gave him a startled glance. He was watching her and smiling, but there was real yearning in his eyes. She looked quickly away, her heart bumping uncomfortably.

Don't, she thought. Not here. Not when her defenses were all scattered and overextended. Everything about him tugged at her senses. If she had to spend much more time with him, it wouldn't matter that he was a big-time ladykiller and way out of her league. She'd be begging him to wreck her life.

She quickened her steps to reach the safety of the food tables and to see Olivia's familiar face. "How's it going, Liv?" she asked unsteadily.

"Great! Betsy, meet Warren and Randall. Offense and defense." Olivia's two admirers each shook Betsy's hand. While they were greeting Jesse, Olivia said in a Jimmy Cagney aside, "Betsy, what are you doing here?"

"Paying the price of gullibility," she replied in an undertone. "Say you need me."

Olivia widened her eyes in mock incredulity. "You think I'm nuts? I've got a good thing going." Louder, in a saccharine tone, she said, "We're fine, Betsy. Why don't you just circulate for old times' sake?"

As Betsy glared at Olivia, she was aware of Jesse's amusement. He had more allies on her staff than she did.

"Mom!" From across the field Tad spotted her and sprinted over. "I thought you weren't going to be here! Come and meet my friends."

She let Tad drag her by the hand. Jesse excused

himself and caught up with them. "Good. I wanted you to meet the Tanners. Hap's one of my closest friends."

He made the introductions. "Skippy and Blaine Tanner, and their mother, Sandra. Meet Betsy Carmody. That's Hap in the middle of the touch football game. Sandra, see what you can do to entertain Betsy, will you? I've failed miserably. Come on, Tad. Let's join the game."

Sandra, a small, mahogany-colored woman with a beautiful smile, offered Betsy her hand. "A pleasure to meet you, Betsy. Our boys really like your son. I hope you'll let him come to our house sometime."

"Of course," Betsy murmured, feeling herself pulled a little further into involvement with the team.

"We've been hearing a lot about you from Jesse. I would love to take one of your classes sometime."

"Molly Collins is coming to next week's class. You might enjoy that one too."

"I'll come, then. You get so stale, cooking for children all the time." She smiled broadly.

Betsy couldn't help smiling back. She liked this woman.

"Hap wasn't with the team three years ago, was he, Sandra?"

"No, they got him in a trade two years back." Sandra went on to explain the politics of the situation—the three veterans ahead of Hap in his previous lineup, and San Francisco's need for a good receiver. Betsy listened and responded appropriately, but she watched Jesse out of the corner of her eye. Her forehead furrowed with the confusion she felt as he went down, laughing, under six giggling, triumphant little bodies.

This was the Jesse Kincaid she'd heard and read about for years, wasn't it? The one who drove a silver Jaguar and filled it with beautiful women, who went skiing every year in Switzerland and surfing in Hawaii? She knew he made more money than any football player in history and arrogantly claimed he was the best quarterback in the game. She'd seen him in action snatching away cameras.

But here was a casual man who was loved by kids and respected by his teammates. He made her laugh even when she didn't want to, and he turned her insides to warm honey. She couldn't figure him out.

Seeing the direction of Betsy's gaze, Sandra said gently, "Jesse's quite a man, isn't he?"

"Yes, I suppose he is," Betsy said, sounding more worried than admiring.

When Sandra laughed, Betsy looked down into her warm, wise brown eyes "You're just like me," Sandra confided. "I thought nothing could get me involved with a football player. All that macho high life stuff? Un-uhn!" She shook her head emphatically. "Then along comes Hap, and he's so fine a man, what could I do?" She sighed in contented resignation and smiled conspiratorially at Betsy.

"You're lucky, with Hap," Betsy said. "I once thought I'd never get involved with a football player, and I would've been smart to stick to that plan. Brian was a good football player and a rotten husband, and I have a feeling Jesse's more like him than Hap. According to the papers, he's been through more women than Bluebeard."

"Well, that's because he doesn't like to lead people on," Sandra explained earnestly. "If he doesn't take anyone out more than a few times, they can't make emotional claims on him."

"Or bring paternity suits."

"Betsy, how cynical you are!"

Betsy bit her lip, feeling ashamed. "Sorry. Maybe I'm wrong about him, but I've learned the hard way to watch out for fast-living, sweet-talking men. Besides, he scares me a bit. He pushes me around every time I see him."

"And you have to push back to keep from falling," Sandra said dryly.

Betsy looked indignant. "To keep from being squashed." Sandra just smiled.

Betsy glanced back at the game. A hopeful young lovely with long Farrah Fawcett curls had joined in and was flashing brilliant white teeth at Jesse. The spiral of tension at the base of Betsy's neck wound a notch tighter. If she did allow herself to get involved with Jesse, how long could it last with competition like that coming in waves?

Jesse eventually left the game, sweat rolling down the side of his face. Sandra reached into a cooler for a soft drink and handed it to him with a laugh. "Here, you look like you could use this."

"Thanks." Jesse reached for the can with one hand and for Betsy's fingers with the other. His skin was moist and cool. Her gaze fastened in helpless fascination on the shirt clinging damply to his chest as he took a long swig of soda.

He set the can down on the cooler. "Come on, Betsy, we're going to dance. Excuse us, Sandra."

"See what I mean?" Betsy complained over her shoulder as Jesse pulled her after him.

Sandra's laughter followed her across the field.

Jesse swung her into his arms. "Alone at last," he teased. "Did you miss me?"

Staring up at the vivid strength of his face, Betsy felt weak. "No," she said unconvincingly.

Chuckling, Jesse pulled her closer, and she allowed him to because he couldn't see her face when it was against his chest. She could feel the vibration of his voice beneath her cheek. "Admit it, you've had some fun after all. You like Sandra, don't you?"

"I like Sandra." Her tone made it clear she was admitting nothing more.

"And it wasn't as bad as you thought?"

"It was worse," she claimed in a small, sullen voice. She knew it wasn't true. It was uncomfortable to be there, but nothing more. But she felt that any admission she made to him would open the door for other, more dangerous admissions.

Jesse's voice held a smile. "Tell the truth," he admonished her, "and don't pout."

Why did he always see through her? She tried to pull away, annoyed. It had as much effect as tugging on a telephone pole. She looked up at him indignantly. "You want the truth? The truth is I don't like you at all."

He knew she was saying darn you, anyway, Jesse Kincaid, why do you know so much?

"And I thought you were a gentle, sweet young thing." He shook his head in mock sorrow. "How disillusioning."

She looked at him like someone who was drowning and beginning to think it was useless to struggle. His gaze roamed her face, and from the look in his eyes she knew what he was thinking as clearly as if he'd said it aloud.

She took a deep breath and held it. His thigh, rock solid and warm, brushed hers. She could feel the moist heat of his shirt. A wave of sensation rolled over her, and she had to look away abruptly to avoid being sucked into the undertow. She felt naked. She felt as if she'd been scalded. She felt terrified at how easily he could control her.

When she could breathe again, she whispered, "Don't change the subject."

He laughed, and pulled her close again. It took all her willpower to keep from leaning into his chest as if it were home.

"You like me," he said over her head, "and someday you're going to admit it."

Six

The dance was a revelation. When Betsy and Jesse finally moved apart and looked at each other, their faces both reflected shock. Jesse's forehead and upper lip were beaded with perspiration, and his chest rose and fell as if he'd been lifting weights. Betsy felt like gelatin dissolved in boiling water.

He weakened her. When he touched her, she forgot her principles, her goals in life, her firmest decisions. She wanted to lay her head on his chest, brush her lips back and forth, relax so that every part of her touched every part of him. What he wanted to do she didn't know, but it was something that tightened his muscles to trembling with the effort at control.

She stared at him, shaking, and thinking there was no mystery about the cause of the headache that was threatening to blow the top of her head off.

When he kept his distance, she could enjoy his personality and hang on to sanity; when he touched her, she was lost. She wanted him more than she'd ever wanted anything, and it was all wrong, and it was scaring her to death. Jesse created so many conflicting emotions in her, it was a wonder she hadn't exploded.

She made an indeterminate little gesture with her hand. "I'd better get to work," she said lamely, backing off.

He knew she was running, of course, but she couldn't help that. She wanted out of there. She wanted to get home and take some aspirin. She needed to think, and she was frantic to put some distance between her and Jesse Kincaid. She wheeled around and set off for the food stations at a trot. Jesse watched her through narrowed eyes before following slowly.

"Ray, why don't you and the others dig in, now," Betsy said. She always urged her staff to eat at some point during a long event. You couldn't ask people to cook and serve food for hours without eating any.

"Sounds good," Ray said. "We're down to a trickle, anyway." Afternoon had faded into evening, and the picknickers were dispersing.

"Yippee, Mom says dig in!" Tad took Betsy's statement as permission for him and Skippy and Blaine to polish off the desserts. In seconds he had a chocolate-cake moustache.

"I'll pack up, Liv," Betsy told her hard-working friend. "Eat and relax for a while."

"Okay," Olivia said cheerfully. "I got three sign-ups for next week's cooking class."

"Great. I got two. That means it'll be a big one."

Olivia filled her plate and sat on the ground with Warren, who had apparently outlasted Randall.

Betsy dragged plastic mesh crates and hor d'oeuvres trays from beneath the long tablecloths. As she straightened, she saw Jesse approaching. She ran a distracted hand through her hair, feeling restless and edgy enough to snarl.

Jesse watched the wind catch strands of Betsy's hair and blow them across her face, checking the impulse to reach out and brush them away. Being near her all afternoon was straining his patience to the breaking point. "I'll help," he offered obligingly.

"You don't need to, I'm not paying you."

"It's free. Gratis. No strings."

She struggled for self-control. "Jesse," she said softly, putting a hand on his arm for emphasis. He looked down at her hand, his expression strained, and she quickly removed it. She couldn't touch him. The aware-ness between them was too strong.

She tried again, sweetly reasonable. "I have had fun today, Jesse. Thank you for that. But now I have work to do, so I'd better say good-bye."

"I told you, I'll help."

"No, thank you." Her control was slipping. That came out almost sharp.

He ignored her. He knew he was just beginning to get to her. He needed time to overcome her resistance, and he'd be damned if he'd trot meekly off. "It's no trouble. What do you do with the salad dishes?"

She struggled with herself for a moment, then said, "Put these lids on them and pile them in the plastic crates."

She worked with silent efficiency, stacking and pack-ing and steadfastly refusing to look at Jesse. He kept pace, watching her with amusement and humming. She recognized the tune. It was a love song. She had to grit her teeth to keep from snapping at him to shut up.

Without a word to him, she hoisted a crate and headed for the truck. He hefted another and followed. By the time they reached the truck, Betsy's nerves were raw. She swore she could feel him behind her with every cell of her body. Why wouldn't he leave her alone? She'd had enough! She had to think!

He put his crate down and reached for hers. She unlocked the truck and watched him slide the crate in. "Just over against that corner," she told him, bending to pick up the second crate.

He stowed his and came out for the next one, smiling and saying, "Yes, boss."

The smile did it—all that warmth and humor, and those damn white teeth. She felt like someone with her back to the wall and a circle of wolves around her. He reached for her crate, but she didn't release it. He looked at her questioningly. Her expression held him immobile. There was no answering smile and no re-sponse in her wide eyes, either. She was pale.

This was it, then. Showdown.

"I'd rather do it myself, Jesse," she said in a low, taut voice.

"Of course you would," he agreed. Neither of them let go of the crate. Betsy's eyes flashed. They were a dark black-green now instead of their usual warm hazel.

She told herself she would not oblige him with an argument. He'd love to make her really mad. He'd been goading her all afternoon, between bouts of subtle seduction. But the less emotion between them, the better for her. Anger, in this case, wasn't all that far from desire.

Enunciating carefully, she said, "This isn't your job, Jesse. I'm uncomfortable having you help me."

"Could you get used to it? I think I'm hooked on it."

"I don't want to get used to it."

He smiled challengingly. "Seemed to me you were starting to settle in back there, in time to the music."

She glared at him, unable to contradict it. Still holding tightly to her self-control, she said, "Why can't you get it? I'm simply not interested in an affair right now."

"How about a friendship?"

"You're about as capable of a platonic friendship as a rabbit."

He grinned. "Where you're concerned, you might be right." His gaze slid over her, underscoring the remark. "But I don't believe you're not interested in an affair. Your body says different."

Her self-control fled in a rush. "Oh, shut up!" she snapped as color flooded her cheeks. "My body doesn't run my life."

His head tilted teasingly to one side. "It's not allowed even a little input?"

"There are bodies littering the planet. Why can't you find one that's willing?"

"I think I have. But in any case, I want the one that goes with your smile."

It was too much for her to handle. Whatever she said he had a comeback. She wanted to scream and throw things, and she couldn't. Her mouth twisted and tears formed in her eyes. Damn! Was she going to cry on top of everything else? She hated crying in front of people.

Jesse's expression changed to concern. He'd pushed her too far, he told himself. This wasn't a football game. "Betsy, what's wrong?" One hand reached toward her cheek. She jerked her head furiously, rejecting his touch before he made contact. He released the crate and shoved his hands into his pockets.

"Please," she said with a touch of desperation, "please back off."

His eyes narrowed. "Are you sure you want me to?"

"You've been crowding me all day." Her voice was husky from the tears she was fighting. "You're still doing it."

"How can you feel so threatened by someone a whole crate away?" he asked, trying to make her laugh. He'd wanted to break through her reserve, but her tears disturbed him more than he could have guessed.

Her brow furrowed in concentration. "I don't know why you're going to all this trouble. You could crook a finger and have all the women you'd ever want."

"It's no trouble. In fact, I doubt if I could stop myself," he said, in a nearly inaudible voice.

Betsy hardly heard him. She continued puzzling aloud, "Is it the challenge? Didn't anyone ever refuse you before?"

She watched his face settle into a stony mask and heard him say, "No one who mattered."

As his comment registered, she made a small sound of helpless, furious protest. "I can't matter to you!"

His mouth twisted. "No?" Then he said, "I'm in love with you."

She gave a little involuntary whimper, and the crate she held crashed to the ground. Jesse didn't flinch at the sound of shattering china. His gaze never left her face.

Why was he doing this to her? Betsy thought wildly. He could have anyone. Why was he saying these things? And why did he sound so sincere? Lust she could understand and deal with. But he was talking about love.

"You don't even know me!" she whispered.

In a low, expressionless voice, he agreed. "Crazy, isn't it? But it's eating me up." The longing came through, even in his quiet, even tones. His shoulders were hunched in tense control.

Betsy drew in a breath with difficulty. She felt a shaking in her limbs and panic circling her brain. As an antidote to both, she stamped her foot. "I'm not. Going. To go out. With you." She accompanied the words with a glare.

The glare he could have handled, even enjoyed. It was the tears rolling down her face that undid him. He couldn't push any more, and she'd refuse any comfort he could offer. It was three years ago all over again. He was still just a glamourboy to her, an annoying stereotype.

His lips compressed in self-mockery. "So you said. About six times, now, counting three years ago. Should be enough even for a dumb jock, right?" He pulled a handkerchief from his pocket and tucked it into her unresisting hand. Then he turned and walked toward the practice fields, hands in his pockets, eyes on the ground.

Betsy stared at his receding back through tears of frustration. Her resistance had been a last-ditch effort. If he hadn't walked off when he did, she'd have screamed one last time and run into his arms.

She should be relieved he'd left and saved her from her own treacherous impulses. But she was feeling like the rope in a tug-of-war. She'd rejected him, and he'd given her a handkerchief before he'd left. What kind of man did a thing like that?

Jesse's brain raced as he forced one foot in front of the other. Had he been kidding himself, thinking she'd really like to open up to him? He understood private people, Lord knows. He was one himself. Nobody with a mother who exploited his every weakness grew up without learning to protect himself.

But people had to share with someone, sometime, didn't they? Or was he just doing a lot of wishful thinking? The fact that he'd found someone he felt was special, didn't mean she had. And yet . . . there was something between them. He was sure she was attracted to him, if only she'd quit fighting it.

He stopped dead. Maybe it wasn't all that different from a football game. Feeling pity for your opponents meant you lost. Un-unh, he decided. If he was going down, he'd go down fighting. His jaw clenched as he turned and retraced his steps.

He watched her eyes widen and her lips part before he stepped around the crate and took her arm. She gasped as she was tugged off balance. His lips covered the sound, and his free hand caught her other arm to steady her against him.

For a moment startled hazel eyes stared into determined brown ones. Jesse's forehead was furrowed, Betsy noted, and there was pain behind the resolution in his eyes. Oh, why did he have to care? she thought as her eyes feathered closed and her resistance evaporated. It made it that much harder.

That was her last coherent thought. Being kissed by Jesse was like being caught in a volcanic eruption. There was a rumble of warning, a moment of panic, then an explosion and molten heat that seared and enveloped her.

Her head fell back under the pressure of his mouth, and she made a little shocked exclamation deep in her throat. Her hands lifted to his sides to feel his rippling muscles. *Jesse!* her mind pleaded.

The force of the kiss was a pale shadow of the forces driving Jesse. He ached for her, and his control had been stretched too thin.

His urge was to excite her into submission. He could do it, he knew, because however hard she shoved him away, she ignited under his hands. Her skin warmed and her body softened. He didn't think it was fear that made her fingers shake as they explored his chest. He knew the attraction was as volatile for her as it was for him.

He kissed her again and again, hard and forcefully, giving her no time to react between kisses. She kissed him back, making short, inarticulate sounds. Her fingers clenched and clutched at him. For both of them, it was a swift and total involvement.

Jesse's hands moved from her arms down under her sweater and up to close over her silk-clad breasts. How he'd longed to touch her this way! When she arched in reaction, he slid one hand to her waist and pulled her close. Her lower body moved against his, instinctively. She was shaking, her breath coming in soft gasps.

Through hot, blurred eyes he studied her. Her skin was delicate, and her waist under his hand was the size of his thigh.

Betsy opened glazed eyes and was captured by his intense stare. When he touched her, she had no resistance. He could do anything he wanted.

Her lips parted and she gazed helplessly at him while his thumb smoothed over her nipple in a feather-soft touch that sent shafts of desire lancing through her body. She moaned and closed her eyes in an agony of pleasure.

Her head dropped backward, offering him the smooth, tempting curve of her neck. He lowered his mouth to her throat, still caressing her, and tasted her skin. It had a wild-honey flavor with just a hint of musk. Under his lips he felt the blood throbbing in her veins. She shuddered in his arms.

Jesse's pulse galloped. He retained just enough sanity to know that he couldn't take her here, and that he had to stop now if he was going to stop at all.

His lips moved to hers and caressed them. He pressed light, tiny kisses from one side of her mouth to the other, until her eyes opened and she looked at him in wonder. He withdrew his hand from under her sweater and held her head to his chest for several minutes, while their breathing steadied and their heartbeats slowed.

Every thought Betsy tried to form popped like a bubble. *I want . . . But he's . . . Why can't I . . . ? What should I . . . ?*

Amusement threaded through Jesse's husky voice as he said, "A cool-down's always a good idea after exercise."

She lifted her head to look at him seriously. "Jesse . . ." she began hesitantly, wanting to explain how she could be saying yes and no at the same time.

He put a finger on her lips. "Shhh," he said. "I've had all the messages I can handle from you today. Verbal and nonverbal."

She opened her mouth to speak, and he bent his head to kiss her, firmly and finally. Then he released her, winked, and walked off. She put unsteady fingers to her lips, still feeling the kiss as she watched him go.

Seven

One morning two weeks after she'd last seen Jesse, Betsy pulled her car to the curb in front of Tad's school. She leaned over for a kiss. " 'Bye, Tadpole."

Tad kissed her noisily before saying reproachfully, "Mo-om!"

"Oops, sorry, I forgot. 'Don't call me Tadpole.' " She ruffled his hair teasingly and got another pleading look from her son. Grinning, she said, "You're going to do it, aren't you? You're going to go and grow up on me. I'll have to call you Theodore."

Tad was an expert at tuning out irrelevant adult comments. From the sidewalk, he said, "Save me something from the chocolate class, okay?"

"Will do. See you at three." She pulled away from the curb and drove off, leaving Tad to make his own way into school.

The blast of a car horn drew her gaze from Tad in the rear-view mirror to the street in front of her. She screeched to a halt several feet beyond the stop sign and made a face. One of these days she'd get killed trying not to be an overprotective mother.

She worked hard at it. Every instinct told her to stay until she saw Tad enter the building—worse, to walk him in. Instead, she drove briskly off and watched him for a block in the rear-view mirror.

When Tad lost his father, she realized one of the things she had to guard against was being overprotective. She didn't want Tad worried and anxious. But children were mirrors, and he would be what she was, having no other model. And with all the responsibility for raising Tad on her shoulders, she didn't always feel as casual and confident as she'd like. She had to fake it sometimes.

So far it was working. Tad faced the world with a smile, but not with a swagger.

That had been her other concern. No son of hers was going to grow up thinking the world was his oyster and the people around him the shuckers. Tad had as much freedom as she could give him, but he also had limits and chores.

She wondered what she should save him from the class. Maybe a slice of the raspberry mousse and a chocolate leaf. Today's class was an important one, so she'd kept it fairly small.

Her mind shifted to last week's class, on spa cuisine. It had really been too big, though fun. She thought Molly and Sandra had enjoyed themselves. A grin spread across her face. Whether their husbands would enjoy the minute, beautifully presented portions of spa food was another question.

Sandra had invited her to dinner. "Will Jesse be there?" Betsy had asked bluntly.

In her forthright way, Sandra had said, "Yes, this time he will. But that's not the only reason I asked you."

Betsy had smiled, grateful for the honesty and the friendliness. "Ask me another time, Sandra, okay?"

Now she shifted into low to take a steep downgrade and wondered again why Jesse hadn't called her for two weeks.

Well, of course he hadn't, she told herself. If ever a man got a rude brush-off, it was he. She'd wanted him to leave her alone, hadn't she? Not even Jesse Kincaid had a big enough ego to come back for more of what she'd dished out at the Miners' picnic. She blocked the memory of the kiss that was the last thing she'd served up.

Rounding the corner of her street, she glanced at a man who was sitting on her top step, pulled into her driveway, did a doubletake, and had to slam on her brakes to keep from going through the gate.

Jesse grinned and nodded amiably at her astonished face.

She watched him get to his feet, moving stiffly. His blue corduroy shirt stretched tight across his shoulders as he protected the bouquet of flowers he held in one hand. Chrysanthemums, the same golden-wheat color as his hair. Damn. A humming gladness in her chest told Betsy she was in trouble.

Jesse opened her car door and held out the mums with a flourish. "Sweets for the sweet," he declaimed. "No, that's wrong, isn't it?" He tried again. "Flowers for the floured. Compliments to the chef." She just stared at him.

"Here, take 'em, for Pete's sake," he commanded. "I'm getting muscle cramps in my fingers."

She took the flowers with a sigh. She couldn't summon a snarl. She was too happy to see him. "Thanks for the flowers, Jesse," she said doubtfully, "but what are you doing here? I have a class in half an hour."

He put on his best offended face. "I'm surprised you have any students if this is how you treat them." As her jaw dropped, he grinned. "I'm moving up from deviled eggs. Broadening myself, you might say." He patted his flat stomach to emphasize the joke.

She groaned. "Sign up for a humor class, instead. You're heavy on the puns today."

He shut the car door behind her. "Next week," he promised. "Today, I'm going for calories. The conditioning coach would croak if he knew what I'm about to consume."

"Who said you'll get to eat it?" she asked, heading for the steps.

"Try and stop me," he challenged, right behind her. "Chocolate does strange things to my self-control. A little like you."

She ignored his remark but turned to him as a thought struck her. "Why aren't you at practice?"

He smiled. "They don't want me. I'm too old."

Her eyes widened. "You were hurt on that third sack two weeks ago." She knew too much about professional football to believe Jesse had just been given a day off. If he was excused from practice, he was hurt.

His smile grew. "Watched the game, did you?"

She tilted her head haughtily, annoyed that she'd given herself away. "My son won't talk to me if I can't talk football." In another tone, she persisted, "What got hurt?"

He reached for the keys she held in her hand and fit one into the keyhole. "It's nothing. A bruise and a twisted ankle." He pushed the door wide and motioned for her to precede him. "The coach isn't taking any chances. He expects to be in the play-offs, and he wants me healthy. Most serious injuries come when you try to play on top of minor ones. Kaplan's doing well enough to win games for us."

He was right. Kaplan had played almost all of the previous week's game. She wondered, fleetingly, if Jesse had decided not to call her because he was injured. No, she decided. If he could hold flowers, he could hold a telephone. But she had an inkling he was the kind of man who holed up when he was hurt. She couldn't see him crying on anyone's shoulder.

She entered the house, then turned to watch him close the door. He looked thicker than usual in the middle.

"What's this, then?" she asked, putting a hand to his rib cage.

"Ow!" It was a completely involuntary yelp, and he winced away from her hand. She looked at him accusingly, feeling an angry concern.

"If you want to explore my anatomy, I can think of places I'd rather have you start," he said indignantly.

"Stupid masochist!" She breathed through her nose with annoyance at the things people did for money, then turned and stalked toward the kitchen.

He followed, a pleased smile on his face. "Betsy, you care," he said with exaggerated surprise.

Her mouth twitched. In the kitchen she found a vase and filled it with water for the flowers. She set them in the middle of the table, thinking how well they complemented the wood.

"I should make you wait on the steps," she murmured, twitching the blossoms into place. "I've got lots to do." She took off her cardigan and pulled a chef's apron over her head, reaching behind to tie it around her slim waist.

Jesse's eyes followed her every move. "How can anyone look so good in an apron?"

She rolled her eyes warningly but couldn't help smiling. "Behave," she ordered.

"Good as gold," he promised, selecting a stool.

Betsy walked over to one of the enormous refrigerators and opened the door. For at least a minute she stood staring, taking in the fact that it was as warm in the cavity as it was in the room. Then she grabbed for her mocha torte, suddenly galvanized into action. "Oh, no!" she wailed. She looked at the runny mess that was supposed to be glassy-smooth chocolate glaze, and at the amorphous lumps that had once been molded chocolate leaves.

"What's wrong?" Jesse asked, rising from his stool.

She deposited the torte on the table and dived back into the refrigerator for a chocolate-rum charlotte, which jiggled in the center where it should have been solid. She deposited the confection by the torte, before whirling around to find the electric outlets.

She bent down and came up with the detached plugs to the refrigerators, waving them wildly in the air. "It's Alex, the little horror. I'll kill him. I've told him and told him!"

"He unplugged the refrigerators?" Jesse asked incredulously.

She nodded. "He cleans up in here once a week, and he likes to listen to music. He unplugs the refrigerators to plug in the vacuum cleaner and his tape deck. I've warned him a thousand times about replugging them. Oh, why didn't I check them last night?"

Jesse frowned. "Why don't you tell him to use some other outlet?"

"These are the only ones near the floor. He once used the one above that counter, and practically destroyed everything on top of it as the cord dragged back and forth."

"But is it crucial?" he asked. "You're going to make these things again for the class, right? So you'll be able to display the finished products?"

"No," she said mournfully. "Each of these desserts has several steps. The charlotte, for instance, has to be refrigerated several hours before it cuts properly. Same for the mousse. Besides, I can't glaze the mousse until it's cold and properly set. The desserts we actually serve have to be finished, or at least started, the day before. And this torte's hopeless." She gestured dramatically at the oozing chocolate glaze.

Betsy delved into the hotbox again. "My leaves!" She held up a plastic bag full of limp vegetation. "They're supposed to be pretty, and cold enough to harden melted chocolate when it's brushed on them."

Completely without sympathy, Jesse said, "Tell 'em never to make this cake during a power outage."

He was rewarded with a weak giggle. "I'll bet you laugh at funerals."

"You should write a book. Between the garbage collectors and Alex, you lead an exciting life."

She pretended to consider his idea. "There was the time the cat ate part of a wedding cake. We didn't see him do it so we weren't sure how it had happened, but we patched up the cake and delivered it. When we found the cat with whipped cream all over his whiskers, we called up and confessed. All the wedding guests were furious."

Jesse roared, thumping the table. "Ow," he wailed, still laughing and holding his ribs. "Dont make me laugh. It hurts." Betsy had to laugh, too.

Between chuckles, Jesse said, "You've got to write a book. We should handle this crisis on the basis of what would make good story material."

"We could run out and buy food samples from my closest competitor."

"You could send the students to pick leaves. Call it culinary field work."

"We can claim the mousse is a new creation. Chocolate soupple."

Jesse hooted. "Or you can paint me with chocolate, peel it off, and call it chocolate moose."

They both groaned at that one. "Your humor's on a level with Tad's today." Betsy wiped tears of laughter from her eyes with her apron.

The phone rang. She stared at it, wondering what else could go wrong. After three rings, Jesse lifted the receiver and handed it to her with a quirk of one eyebrow. "The phone, madam," he said in his best butler's voice.

She lifted it to her ear gingerly. "Hello?" she said. Jesse watched her brow furrow as she strained to make sense of the noise coming over the line.

"Liv?" Betsy asked doubtfully. "Is that you? You don't sound like yourself." Her mouth opened in consternation as she listened again. "Oh, no!" A pause. "No, no, it's nothing. Don't worry, it'll be all right. You just get to bed and take care of yourself." Her calm, reassuring voice was at odds with her worried face. "I'll find someone to fill in. Go to bed, do you hear? I'll call in a while to see what you need. Drink tea. I'll talk to you later." She replaced the receiver slowly.

"Olivia's sick," Jesse surmised. "Does that affect you?"

Betsy bit her lip and nodded. "I don't know if I can teach the class without an assistant. I could get one of the students to hand me things, but someone has to wash dishes as we go to keep me in beaters and spatulas."

Jesse smiled widely and spread his arms, palms up, in a gesture of offering. "You might not believe this," he said with mock humility, "but I myself have had intensive training in the fine art of washing dishes. And I do know butter from cream."

She smiled tentatively. "I can't ask you to wash kitchen utensils."

"Who asked? I'm offering. I'm begging. This may be my big chance to prove myself to you."

Her lips were tugged into an answering smile, which faded almost immediately. She put her hands to her hot cheeks as she felt panic return. "I can't teach this class! For what they're paying, these people expect a smooth, high-class act, not stand-up comedy!"

Jesse took three steps and put his hands on her shoulders. "Life is comedy," he said gently. "They'll love it."

She looked up at him, and his eyes crinkled. "I'll love it." He could feel her relaxing under his hands. "We're going to have a good time."

"You're right," she agreed. "I don't know why I'm getting into such a state. Maybe because someone from the paper is coming to check me out today. I'm one of the candidates for a position as columnist in their new weekly food section. But I shouldn't be in this business if I can't handle crises."

"You'll handle it." He squeezed her shoulders before he stepped away. "So don't stand there moaning, girl. Plug in the refrigerator. We've got work to do. Do you have a freezer that's functional?"

She did a quick check and nodded. "Yes, Alex didn't unplug that."

Jesse was stripping the leaves from a chrysanthemum stalk. "Good thing these are fresh. Here, stick 'em in the freezer for a few minutes. Maybe you could even stiffen up the raspberry mousse and the rum charlotte that way?"

She looked at him, surprised that he even knew what a charlotte was, then nodded. She was too relieved at having some constructive suggestions to quibble. "Thank goodness I haven't garnished them yet."

"Do you have any of these cakes at one of the shops?"

"It's a torte, but yes, at Calcuisine, on Union."

"I'll go get a replacement, then. Will that do it? Can we fake the rest?"

"I think maybe we can," she said slowly, and looked at him with relief and growing wonder. Her eyes were luminous and her mouth soft.

"Right," he said quickly. "Be back soon. Keep your apron on."

On the way down the front steps, he muttered, "And don't look at me like that again if you don't want to be kissed."

Betsy packed the last wedge of mocha torte in a green-latticed Calcuisine container and presented it to Vernon Curtin. "There you are. Enjoy it."

The editor from the *Herald* gave her a smile that made him look like an oversized cherub. "I will," he promised. "I enjoyed the class. Extremely innovative and very entertaining." Betsy smiled in gratification and relief.

Vernon Curtin held his hand out to Jesse. "And I enjoyed meeting you, Mr. Kincaid."

"My pleasure," Jesse replied. "I'll look forward to reading your article next week."

As the door closed behind Vernon Curtin, Betsy sagged against it. "Hooray," Jesse said. "Restrained cheers and cries of relief."

"Amen," Betsy said in heartfelt tones. She pried herself off the door. "I think it was a success."

"Of course it was." How could anyone spend four hours looking at Betsy and not consider the day a success? He didn't think she realized she was a born teacher. She incorporated amusing anecdotes and gentle witticisms into her presentation, and she made a point of helping and talking to each person individually. She hadn't lost the class's interest for a second.

"You're an amazing hostess," he told her quietly. "You made everyone here feel special."

She blushed in surprised pleasure and typically tried to brush off the compliment. "You helped a lot, Jesse. I appreciate it."

"Right," he agreed promptly. "I was terrific. In fact, you'd find me an asset in many areas of your life." She tilted her head and looked up at him sideways. Give him an inch . . .

He had been wonderful, though. He seemed to know what she needed before she asked. He presented cream, blocks of chocolate, and fresh measuring cups with quiet efficiency and an occasional flourish that kept the students entertained. Once he'd played surgical nurse, saying, "Chocolate, Cream," as one would say, "Scalpel. Syringe."

Just the spectacle of Jesse Kincaid whisking away the dirty dishes and returning clean ones was enough to fascinate most of the students. Betsy wondered how much of their attention was actually on the cooking techniques.

"You were a great help," she said teasingly, "when you weren't trying to do me in. Was that a snort I heard when I introduced the 'carefully washed and refrigerated' chrysanthemum leaves?"

He grinned. "Well, it was an unmistakable snort you came back with. You'd never have passed it off as a sneeze if I hadn't handed you a tissue."

"With such solicitude you almost set me off again."

They both chuckled, remembering the scene. It wasn't the only time they'd had to avoid each other's eyes to stave off a fit of the giggles. Come to think of it, Betsy realized, she'd never enjoyed a class as much.

She looked at her watch. She'd have to get Tad soon.

Jesse watched her thoughtfully. "Betsy," he said gently, drawing her attention back to him. "I'll ask you one more time, and then I'll quit bothering you."

He wasn't smiling any more. Her eyes widened in apprehension. He was going to give her an ultimatum, and she didn't know if she could say no this time. Not if it was her last chance.

"Will you go out to dinner with me this weekend? I'd ask you for tonight, but I have to work in the emergency room."

Relief washed over her. She couldn't go this weekend, so she didn't have to decide.

She wanted to see him again, she had to admit that much, but if she went out with him . . . On some level she knew that as soon as they were alone together, they'd be lovers. They simply would. The chemistry between them was too potent.

"I can't, Jesse." He was looking at her searchingly, and she rushed on. "I've been invited to a seminar this weekend at the Napa Hoffsgrove Winery. It's something I've wanted to do for a long time, an intensive study of how to match foods and wines. I think it may help my chances of getting the food column."

He nodded. A thought struck her. "Won't you be out of town this weekend? The game's in D.C., isn't it?"

"I told you they don't want me. Coach Paulson said I don't need to go. Maybe they're phasing me out."

Her lips tightened. If he wasn't even making the trip, his injuries were more serious than he was admitting. She discovered she didn't like to think of him in pain. "You can imagine you're fooling me if it makes you happy," she said caustically.

"Take care of yourself, will you?" she added more gently.

"I'll treat myself like a million-dollar investment," he said with a touch of irony.

When she looked at him curiously, he smiled enigmatically and said, "I'll walk out with you."

She collected her purse and locked the house.

Jesse opened the door to her car. With one foot in, she turned to him, feeling that the situation was unresolved. "Thanks again, Jesse, for all your help."

He smiled. "You're welcome."

She remained looking at him. He waited. On impulse, she removed her foot from the car and stood on tiptoe, balancing with one hand atop the car door, to press her lips to his. He remained absolutely motionless, except for an instinctive movement of his mouth. When she drew away, reluctantly, there was a flicker of something in his eyes.

"I didn't do it for the reward," he said steadily.

"I know," she said softly, and reached up to kiss him again. She balanced herself with her hands on his chest, gently, to keep from pressing any of his injuries.

Previously, Jesse had kissed her. This time, she kissed him, nibbling gently on his lower lip with her teeth, teasing the inner edges with her tongue. He dragged breath into his lungs and clenched his fists to keep from hauling her fiercely against him.

Betsy's eyes closed as she centered all her attention on Jesse's mouth. He tasted of chocolate. She placed, kiss after kiss on his lips, pressing just enough to arouse. Then she teased him with her tongue, hinting at deeper, darker intimacies.

She wasn't thinking. She couldn't have said why she was doing this. It was just something that happened as a natural result of her feelings for him after their day together. It had started as a simple expression, or admission—she wasn't sure which—of feeling, but it was changing to something else.

She stepped back with a gasp seconds before Jesse could reach for her. Quickly she whirled around and into the car, closing the door. Coming slowly out of the spell of her kisses, Jesse reacted by grabbing the frame of the open car window. "Get back here," he said as she turned the ignition key. The car coughed to life. "You can't do that." His eyes were flaming now.

She gave a tantalizing, gusty little laugh as she put the car into gear and reversed down the driveway. " 'Bye," she called out provocatively.

Behind her in the driveway, Jesse roared, "Dammit, Betsy! This is the last time you're driving away from me."

She smiled as she waved, but inside she thought he was probably right. It was getting harder and harder to say no to him. It wouldn't be long before she'd be saying please.

Eight

Jesse rolled down his car window. The sun on his bare forearm and the wind on his face felt good. He breathed deeply, smelling the musty odor of grapevines after harvest.

That had to be one of the prettiest places on earth, he thought, admiring the vineyards coating the floor of the Napa Valley and rising gently up the hills on each side. Sunlight bathed the eastern slopes, but dark-green shadows were creeping over the valley floor. Birds chirped randomly.

He smiled, wondering what Betsy would say when she saw him at Hoffsgrove. Something like, "Treacherous snake," probably, but if he was lucky she'd smile when she said it. He just hoped she'd think he wangled an invitation after hearing about hers. If she realized that he'd talked Fred Hoff into inviting her, it might be a slight blow to her pride.

He felt he was making progress with Betsy. She'd kissed him, pouring a potent sensuality into the kiss, and he'd been putting no pressure on her at all. So, he asked himself, was that a yes, or a no? Not quite a yes, he decided, but definitely not a no.

He reached into his traveling ice chest for a bottle of

seltzer a; twisted off the cap. Tilting his head back he took a long swallow.

What a little siren she was, he thought admiringly. Sweetness and quiet warmth on the surface, fire and passion two inches down. And rock-hard integrity and determination underneath it all.

Jesse could have had any number of warm, lovely women. But he wanted more than just sex. He'd been starved for closeness all his life, and now he wanted a depth of intimacy he knew was rarely found between two people. Only the level of emotion he felt for Betsy and sensed in her would satisfy him. He understood her—the private person with the public face. He thought she was capable of understanding him.

In his own way, he thought, startled by the idea, he was as greedy as his mother. He took another drink of the seltzer and rolled it around meditatively in his mouth, thinking about his mother. She didn't look old enough to be his mother. Her hair was still more blond than silver. She would have been beautiful except for a certain coldness in her expression. He realized most people thought she was beautiful.

She'd been a young widow just like Betsy. He shook his head at the thought of how different they were. They'd both built successful businesses. But Betsy put Tad first. His mother had taken control of her husband's stock-brokerage firm and never looked back. For Jessica Kincaid, the business had had no competition in her life. She wanted the best of everything, and she was single-minded enough to build a financial empire that allowed her to have it. If Jesse got neglected in the process, well, growing up was tough sometimes.

The irony of it was that in her quest for total control of her life, she'd ignored him, and now he was the only thing she didn't control. His being a football player hadn't been part of her plan.

He could never be a glutton for control like his mother was, Jesse knew, but he just might be as much a glutton for perfection. That was what Betsy was for him—physical and personal perfection.

What was it about her beauty, he wondered, that fired him so much more than any other woman? In his mind he saw her: Far-away, thickly-fringed eyes that held such secrets, then looked at a child and warmed to golden laughter; the sensitivity of her mouth, so vulnerable and so sensual. Just the parting of her lips could start his heart hammering hard enough to hurt.

All his life Jesse had been able, without effort, with simply a touch, to have women clutching and crying out. He played his part well, and he always thought, is that all there is to it?

Somehow he'd known there had to be a woman who could do for him what he did for others. He had suspected Betsy was the one. One kiss and he had been sure. He had years of banked passion waiting for her.

His hand tightened on the steering wheel, bringing a quick twinge of pain to his chest muscles. He could hardly drive a car, much less throw a football.

The injuries were turning out to be a boon, though, in some ways. He wanted Betsy to see him in an environment other than football. If he hadn't been hurt, he wouldn't have had time. He smiled with a ruthlessness his mother would have recognized. He was going to make the most of this weekend.

Betsy leaned on the railing of the Hoffsgrove House veranda, letting the cocktail-hour babble behind her fade from her consciousness, and concentrated on the view. Directly below her were sweeps of green lawn dotted with magnolia and sycamore trees and bordered by clumps of hydrangea, bottlebrush, and oleander. Farther down the hillside, the vines cast long shadows, turning the vineyards into alternating stripes of darkness and red or gold autumn foliage. Above, the sun illuminated just the tips of trees on the crest of the hill.

She swirled the champagne in her glass to watch the bubbles shake loose and break the surface. Inhaling deeply, she thought of how long it had been since she'd taken the time to enjoy the twilight and breathe country air. What would she be doing if she'd stayed in the city? Cooking, probably, and talking to Tad.

But maybe she'd have been sitting down to a meal with Jesse. Would she? she asked herself. If she hadn't had plans, would she have gone?

Maybe, she decided, smiling a slow, secret smile. He'd been charming and helpful lately, showing none of that high-handed, super-macho stuff. She might have had a quick dinner with him.

She ignored the jeering voice in her head that demanded, and afterward? You'd have told him good-bye and he'd have trotted off like a good little boy? Sure.

Betsy wondered where Jesse was eating, and if he was alone. She told herself she was glad she was here and not there. At least she was relaxing. If they'd gone out together, she'd have been on a roller-coaster from one emotion to another. She wouldn't have been able to look at the vineyards or concentrate on the lectures. When Jesse was around, he filled her mind and senses.

She hoped he was taking care of his ribs. He got plenty of attention for his ailments, no doubt, but did anybody really care how he felt? Was he ever lonely?

Angry with herself for her obsessional thoughts, she straightened away from the railing and took a determined sip of champagne. 'Eighty-one. A good year, she recited mentally, reviewing the day's lessons.

Behind her Vernon Curtin's full, ringing voice said, "Ah, Bettina, there you are. We were discussing the benefits of European training for chefs. I still can't believe you've created an entirely new cuisine without any continental experience. Remarkable." It would have been a compliment, except for the dubious, challenging tone of his voice.

Betsy pasted a smile on her face and turned, sighing inwardly. This had to be the longest ongoing interview on record. She'd endured two hours of grilling while driving up with Vernon, and now he was at it again. Was he thorough, or did he just enjoy needling people?

She sipped her champagne before answering. "Actu-

100 · SUSAN RICHARDSON

ally, I think it's easier to work creatively without years of rigid training to set your mind in a particular cast. But maybe I am handicapped and don't even know it." She smiled amiably, thinking if she had to put up with many more of his remarks she'd tell him to take his column and stew it.

Curtin's round, baby face was blank. She'd stolen his ammunition, and he didn't know what to say.

When his expression turned from sulky to perky, Betsy glanced behind her to see what he was looking at. A car was winding its way through the terraced vineyards. It caught a last gleam of sunlight, and threw back a silver reflection.

She stiffened and followed the Jaguar with her eyes until it pulled into a parking slot below the veranda. She watched as a man with a golden head and broad shoulders eased himself out of the car.

Vernon drawled in malicious glee, "Ah, it's your pet celebrity, Bettina."

Betsy hardly heard him as anger and happiness struggled within her. How dare he? was her first thought. How dare he follow her like this? But then a singing gladness coursed through her as she honestly admitted, at last, that this was what she wanted. All her caution, all her self-preservation, was useless. Just the sight of him, and her resistance evaporated. They'd be lovers tonight. She couldn't— wouldn't—fight him any longer.

Below her, Jesse slung a garment bag over his shoulder, wincing. As he looked up, sensing her there, their gazes locked. Betsy's eyes were wide and unwavering. A current passed between them that lifted the hairs on the back of her neck.

Jesse's eyes narrowed in predatory appraisal. Betsy had never looked more beautiful. Her hair was swept up and held back with combs, accentuating the purity of her profile. She wore a peach-colored top in a thin, silky knit fabric and a long printed skirt in the same shade. Her breasts rose and fell quickly with her breathing. He could feel the passion emanating from her. Thank heavens, he thought, staring.

She looked both regal and soft. She was all the contradictions that made him love her. He didn't know if he could wait until after dinner. His nostrils flared as he dragged oxygen into his lungs.

Betsy saw desire in his eyes. He had no smile for her tonight, and no charm. He didn't need them.

Beside her Vernon Curtin lifted his hand to wave to Jesse, then dropped it in a vague, incomplete gesture, realizing Jesse hadn't even seen him. He was completely focused on Betsy.

Her eyes glittering, Betsy raised her champagne glass in a salute full of meaning before tossing back her head and draining it.

Jesse saw the ripple along her throat and felt heat spread throughout his body.

At the last drop, she turned away from him to hold her glass out to Curtin. "Vernon, would you mind getting me some more champagne?"

Vernon took the glass with a stuttering assent and trotted off. Jesse watched Betsy turn back to him. She stood outlined against the fading light, gazing down. He stared, his mouth dry, until Fred Hoff appeared and said, "Jesse, I'm glad you made it! Come on up."

It took Jesse five minutes to change into a dinner jacket. He made it down to the veranda in time to intercept Vernon Curtin and appropriate Betsy's refilled champagne glass. "Good evening," he said to the open-mouthed food editor. "I'll deliver this."

Betsy watched him thread his way through the crowd. Though his size dwarfed everyone there, his face, with its sculptured planes, aquiline nose, and dangerously intelligent eyes, didn't look like anyone's stereotype of a football player. He didn't look like a stereotype of anything to her anymore. He was just Jesse. He handed her the champagne, and smiled. "Try not to guzzle this glass. Fred's wines deserve better."

"What are you doing here, Jesse?" She was pretending indignation, but her expression was one of pure gladness.

"I told you I wanted to have dinner with you tonight."

"Ahh," she said softly, but her eyes said more—much more.

Jesse took her slim, warm hand in one of his and stroked it lazily with his thumb. Nerves tingled under Betsy's skin.

"Would you have come if you'd known I'd be here?" he asked her directly.

Her gaze dropped to her hand in his. She didn't have to consider the answer. The time for running was over. In a low voice, she said, "Yes."

When Jesse's hand clenched convulsively on hers, she glanced up to see fierce joy in his eyes. Shyly and sweetly she smiled.

He lifted his free hand to touch her cheek. She closed her eyes with a sigh, leaning into his caress. He studied her defenseless face, feeling gratitude and a sudden, powerful sense of responsibility. He resolved she'd never have cause for regret. Not for a second, if he could help it.

Dinner in the firelit Victorian dining room, with its paneled redwood ceiling, moiré wallpaper, and table set with crystal and silver, was a glittering affair.

Another time Betsy would have been fascinated by the mixture of people in the room. There was a French vintner, very debonair and charming, a bejeweled older lady in purple satin, a plain, horsy lady with a low, lovely voice, two young honeymooners, a weatherbeaten rancher, and a smooth, well-groomed chef from a famous northwestern restaurant, among others. Fred Hoff had eclectic tastes in people.

Jesse, to her right, was apparently relaxed. He had leaned back in his chair, one arm over the back, the other outstretched on the table, twirling the stem of his wineglass. She could feel impatience simmering inside him.

Across the table the French vintner smiled at her. "So you are really a chef, Meez Carmody." His voice expressed as much doubt as Vernon Curtin's, but with much more charm. "This is a novel idea for me. In France, cuisine is still very much a man's affair."

"You probably have as many fine female chefs as male ones," she said. "I've met a few of them. It's just that you call them cooks and they don't attend the classical schools. I doubt if I'd be called a chef in France. In fact, I don't actually call myself that."

"Ah-h-h. What, then, do you call yourself?" It was a Gallic flirtation rather than a request for information.

Jesse knew what it was. His dangerous stare was directed across the table at the Frenchman. He felt like a time bomb, sitting next to Betsy, breathing her wild-flower scent. He was in no mood to watch her flirt with distinguished foreigners.

"We call her a creative genius," he stated with near belligerence.

The Frenchman looked taken aback, and Betsy hastened to soften the blow. "That's a bit more than an exaggeration," she said with a light laugh. "I call myself a cooking teacher, actually, and I'd like to think I'm an innovator."

The Frenchman lifted his wineglass to her. "I'm quite sure you deserve your friend's high praise," he said before turning to his dinner partner.

Without looking at Jesse, Betsy murmured, "Don't smash any cameras for me, Jesse. I can defend my own reputation."

He smiled humorlessly and without turning his head replied, "Your culinary reputation, yes. It's your personal reputation he and I were discussing."

He lifted his glass from the table, then set it back down with a crack. Betsy looked quickly at him and heard him mutter explosively, "Damn Fred and his interminable hospitality!"

She echoed the sentiment. So far there'd been four leisurely courses, and no sign of an end.

A maid in a lacy white apron cleared Betsy's untouched plate of green-peppercorn chicken. A young man replaced it with an enormous garden salad. Betsy stared at the beautiful food without interest.

She tasted nothing. After a few bites of the first course, she'd given up eating, and just sipped the wine that accompanied each course. She floated in a curious limbo, the effect half because of the wine, half because of Jesse. It was a little like having a fever, with alternating periods of shivering and burning. It was also a little like dreaming, except that her dreams had never been so erotic.

She felt her body more acutely than ever before. She was aware of the silk jersey brushing her breasts, the skirt sliding across her calves and thighs. She moved slowly to experience it all.

Jesse sensed this new languor in her movements. Wanting her was a throbbing in his loins, an ache in his blood.

He wasn't engineering what was happening between them any longer. It was a little like riding the rapids: there was no turning back. The most he could hope for was to guide the raft.

He noticed that he was drumming his fingers on the table and gripped his wineglass again to stop himself.

It was a real effort to respond when Fred called from the head of the table, "Jess, what's your opinion on this in-the-grape fermentation method Jules is talking about?"

Betsy listened for a minute to Jesse's answer, feeling excitement just from the sound of his voice and wondering how he knew so much about winemaking.

Her dinner partner on her other side was occupied for the moment, relieving her of any social obligations. She stared out the open window at the thick mist that swirled around the valley oaks in the garden, creating mysterious pockets of invisibility.

A lover. She tried the words for size. *I'm about to take a lover.*

She shivered in anticipation. Maybe there would be pieces to pick up tomorrow, but tonight she didn't care. Tonight she was on fire, and it would take a lot more than old tears and current fears to put the flames out. Tonight she'd love Jesse with all the skill and feeling she was capable of, and not think about the future.

Close to her ear Jesse's deep voice asked quietly, "What do you see out there?"

She looked at him, aching to touch the smile creases at the corners of his eyes. It really didn't matter what she said, they were talking with their eyes.

"It's like a thin potato soup," she murmured.

"Don't you ever think about anything but food?" Amusement and a hint of exasperation colored his voice. Food was the last thing on *his* mind.

She looked up at him with a small, provocative smile. "It's one of the basics of life."

"There are other appetites." His gaze fastened on her face and his voice dropped an octave. "But if you want to stick to food, all right. Myself, I can't think of anything but skin like whipped cream, hair like autumn chestnuts, breasts like molded pudding, legs like a long, cool drink of water."

Her breath caught in her throat. His words were corny, on a par with "eyes like diamonds," but his voice more than his words shook her to her core. He was a famished man, and her own hunger growled in her belly.

"Stop it," she whispered.

"I can't. I don't want to. I've waited long enough."

"I'm leaving, then," she said in a choked voice.

For a moment, he just stared at her, his eyes black in a pale face. Then he slowly stood to hold her chair.

He watched her walk to the head of the table, excuse herself to Fred, and leave the room. He stared for at least a minute at the door through which she'd disappeared.

• • •

It had been an hour. Betsy had showered, put on a nightgown, and was now pacing the floor. Maybe he wasn't coming. Maybe she'd be a disappointment to him. Maybe she was making a terrible mistake. All the doubts blotted out by the sight of him made a brief, tormenting reappearance. Let him come soon, she thought, so she could be sure again.

In her mind she pictured Jesse's eyes, and his smile. She felt again his hands on her body and shivered, her doubts retreating. She wasn't marrying him, she told herself. She was just snatching the chance of a joy greater than anything she'd ever experienced. Surely that was worth a few risks.

She shut off the light, lit candles, turned back the sheets on the high Victorian bed, and drifted to the window. She held back the lace curtains with one hand, staring out. It was thick potato soup out there now.

She watched the mists swirl, revealing an oleander lit from the drawing-room window, then erasing it. Her mind stilled and emptied. The time for questioning had passed.

As the knob on the door began to turn, she held her breath and slowly turned her head.

Nine

Standing in the doorway, Jesse looked at the picture of loveliness Betsy made. Shadows and highlights from the candles played over her. One hand was demurely holding onto the lacy curtain, but the expression on her face as she looked over her shoulder was purely provocative. Her gown was cream satin with broad straps, deep v's in front and back, and flowing lines that outlined every curve faithfully. He could see the dimples in the cheeks of her buttocks. Dear Lord!

He closed the door behind him and leaned against it. Beyond the smoldering sensuality and the alluring pose, he noticed there was a stiffness about Betsy. She was clutching the curtain, actually.

Going to her, he lifted a hand to cup the side of her head. She turned her face helplessly and kissed it. He combed his fingers into her hair, which she wore loose now, and lowered his head to brush her lips with his.

"Hi," he said teasingly. "Waiting for someone?"

She drew and expelled a quick breath. "Don't say anything, Jesse. It wouldn't take much to talk me out of this."

"How much would it take to talk you all the way into it?" he murmured against her lips with gentle irony. Without waiting for a response, he increased the pressure on her mouth, moving his hands from her hair to her dangling wrists then sliding them smoothly to her upper arms.

He held her lightly while he kissed her, taking his time. Just as before, the touch of his mouth created a quick compliance in Betsy. He felt her relax against him, felt desire rise in her. It could have been an instant conflagration between them; the coals only needed kindling. But having what he'd waited for here in his hands, Jesse felt a new patience. He'd ached for her. He was going to take his time and enjoy every second.

Betsy had never experienced such concentration and awareness in a kiss. Jesse's head was large, his mouth firm, warm—so warm—and knowing. She felt the power in his hands and the sensitivity in his lips. Her tongue welcomed his. They meshed together as Jesse's arms slid to enfold her.

He lifted his head for breath and heard her whisper, "It didn't take much, did it?" With a short laugh he slid a strap off her shoulder. Maybe he didn't have as much patience as he'd thought.

Betsy had none. Before he could slip the second strap down, she reached for his head to draw it to hers. "Oh, Jesse," she said fervently, "I'm so glad you're here." He made a growling sound low in his throat and took her mouth in a quick flare of hunger.

That was all there was of seduction. The currents had been building between them for weeks. Now they were flooding, and the two of them were swept along and under, fighting for breath and control, and drowning.

As Jesse wrapped himself around her, Betsy felt enveloped by his size and solidity and heat. There was no give to his flesh. It was hard, and hot. Her fingers fumbled with the buttons of his shirt in her impatience to touch. Her hands rose to stroke the strong column of his neck, his thick gold hair. It was she who was moaning and tearing at buttons. She gasped, "Jesse . . . let me . . ."

"Anything." He caught her bottom lip between his teeth and caressed it with his tongue. Then he released it to kiss her in short, hot nips, his hands sliding here, there, everywhere, finding her skin no less satiny than her gown.

She was shaking, burning, astounded at the strength of her desire for him. She'd never known a male body could have so much appeal. She wanted to touch him, to know every sensitive spot on his frame. She couldn't uncover him fast enough. She peeled his jacket and shirt together off his shoulders, her breath catching at the sight of the expanse of sharply defined muscles gleaming in the moonlight.

"Jesse," she said on a sigh, "you're so beautiful." Her hands smoothed across his chest, excited by his physical perfection. When his laugh changed midway to a gasp she realized that the purple patch covering half his chest wasn't a shadow, but a bruise. She lifted her hand quickly. "Oh! Why didn't you tell me? You can't . . ."

"I can," he interrupted, laughter threading his voice. "Believe me, I can."

He drew her to him and this time managed to slide her other strap down. He tensed for a moment from the shock of the loveliness before him. Betsy, suddenly feeling shy, put each hand on the opposite shoulder and tucked her chin down.

"Oh, no," he said, gentle laughter now in his voice. He carefully removed her hands. "No more hiding. I knew you were there all along." The gown slid to the floor.

At the tenderness in his voice, she lifted her head to stare at him in a kind of wonder and a sudden complete sense of safety. It was outside her experience of lovemaking, this sweetness, and she stopped to taste it. With Brian, it had been all greed and glut, all aggressive, unleashed selfishness. With Jesse, she felt enough excitement to burst her heart, but there was more.

She relaxed and smiled at him as he studied her with a look almost of awe. "I knew you'd be lovely," he said in a hoarse voice, "but I didn't know you'd be this beautiful. Come here to me."

He held out a hand in demand, and she put hers into it. His patience was stretched to its limit. His mouth took hers with a kiss that was as far beyond seduction as the skillful movements of his hands on her breasts.

Her cry was soundless, but he registered the jerk of her body as sensation shot through her, mobilizing muscles and nerves. She would have staggered if he hadn't swept an arm behind her legs and lifted her. He took three steps to the bed and placed her on it, leaning over her to caress and arouse.

Betsy was shaking, spinning in a whirlpool of sensation she hadn't thought possible. "No," she said, thinking she couldn't stand any more.

"Yes," he answered. He wouldn't stop. This was what he'd thought lovemaking should be. He'd finally found the place of passion and power and rightness he'd been searching for. He knew she was capable of sharing it with him—the heights, the depths. He couldn't stop, and he was taking her with him.

"Jesse!" she cried in protest as his hands and mouth left her. Then, "Jesse," she sighed in satisfaction when he was back, closer and warmer.

She explored all of him with her hands, feeling the textures of his body—the light furring of hair over his hard chest, the ripples of muscles covering his ribs. For Jesse, it was the miracle of breasts and belly, the music of sighs and moans. He put off the consummation as long as he could. He wanted it to last.

When he finally held himself off her, she opened passion-glazed eyes, sensing that he required something of her. Candlelight flickered on his face, which was strained with the necessity of control, yet smiling with intense delight. His chest was rising and falling like a bellows, dragging air into his tortured lungs.

His dark eyes burned into hers, and a sense of wonder again penetrated through the thrumming of her blood. He was reaching out for her. Gone was the arrogance and flamboyance that had made her wary.

All his power was focused on intelligence, generosity, sensitivity. This was a man who wanted to love and share.

She quivered helplessly. Her defenses were down. She couldn't deny him anything. She reached up for his cheek and stroked, an oddly tender gesture in this moment of poised tension.

His laugh of joy and triumph told her it was what he wanted. Still gazing into her eyes he entered her and began to move. As her lashes closed, he heard a long moan, and he lowered his mouth to her throat, feeling gratitude rise up in him along with excitement. She was all he had ever wanted in life.

Betsy was whimpering, groping for the sense of normality she'd left far behind.

"Hold me, Betsy," Jesse commanded as sensation claimed and carried them both through the rapids to crest and plunge in a dizzying waterfall of fulfillment.

Gradually Betsy became aware of candlelight flickering on polished walnut, of breezes from the partially opened window, the smell of grape must from the crush going on all over the valley. She'd never lost her awareness of Jesse's warmth next to her. Her own breathing matched the quiet rise and fall of his chest. He lay on his back to avoid pressing the bruise. She curled against him on her side.

She moved an arm, a bit surprised to find herself fully functional and not shattered into a thousand pieces as she'd imagined. Jesse opened his eyes and turned his head to smile at her.

"Oh, Jesse," she said in gratitude. A wave of emotion washed over her, and she closed her eyes. He'd given her so much. She had found what she had been missing without even knowing it existed, she realized, not just passion, but closeness.

Jesse watched tears seep out from beneath her lashes. He shifted so that he could kiss them away. "Betsy, Betsy," he murmured. "Bettina in the daytime, Betsy in the night." His voice was another kind of loving. He kept kissing her eyelids long after the tears had disappeared.

She sighed, completely satisfied for the moment. She felt totally accepted and totally a woman. For the first time in her life, she felt beautiful and desirable. She wanted Jesse to know what that meant to her. In a hushed, serious voice she groped for words. "That was . . ." She waited for the right phrase. "That was . . . nice," she ended lamely.

He chuckled and she joined in, realizing the total inadequacy of her words. She snuggled closer to him. He knew, without the words. "Yep," he agreed, still amused. "That's what it was."

She smiled in the darkness and ran her hand over his chest. His movement was barely there, certainly not enough to be called flinching, but she lifted her head.

"Does it hurt? You didn't wince earlier."

"I had other things on my mind earlier."

"It did hurt," she accused him.

A laugh gusted out. "Hurt me again."

She wasn't satisfied. "You should have told me, Jesse. You're in no shape for this sort of exercise."

His voice was aggrieved. "Thanks very much. That's the kind of remark it's okay to make before the event, but not afterwards."

She lowered her head to his shoulder. "Tell me where it's all right to touch you."

He laughed again. "What an invitation."

They lay in companionable silence for a time. Betsy stroked Jesse's arm; he lay still, gazing into her eyes.

"Tell me something," she requested lazily. "This macho bit—showing no pain, and all that. Are all men taught that? And is it fathers who teach it? Sometimes I'm afraid I'm not preparing Tad properly for the male world."

"Don't worry about it. It's not necessary for survival. In fact, studying medicine makes it look to me like the macho male's days are numbered. All that suppressed emotion leads to strokes and heart attacks."

"But where does it come from? I was taught to yell like mad when I got hurt."

"In my case it probably came from my mother," he theorized idly. "She didn't believe in pain. One of my earliest memories is of falling out of a big tree—at least it seemed big at the time—and hearing her say, 'Get up, Jesse. You're not hurt.' "

He chuckled, but Betsy was indignant. "That's inhuman!"

"That's my mother. No one's ever accused her of humanity. Fortunately, there was Gracie." His voice softened.

"Who was Gracie?"

"My nanny and the light of my life. Every time Mother said 'Don't cry,' Gracie came bustling along saying, 'But he's hurt, the poor darling.' " He put on an English accent and a smile to imitate Gracie. "I learned that Gracie's rules worked for age ten and under, but Mother's rules went over better after that."

Betsy wondered. Jesse told his story matter-of-factly and with humor. His mother's rigidity obviously wasn't an issue any more, but it couldn't have been easy, growing up with no father and a stern mother.

They lapsed into another silence. Betsy was close to dozing off when Jesse said softly, "Betsy, I want to tell you one thing." She tilted her head to look at his eyes in the flickering light. "I don't believe in hell," he said seriously.

Her eyes closed as she expelled a swift breath, then she opened them. He remembered what she'd told him about life with Brian. Heaven, then hell. It was his way of telling her things weren't going to sour between them.

What a man, she thought. She hadn't known a man could be so strong and caring. If she wasn't careful, she would fall in love with him.

She wanted him to understand. "There are all kinds of hells," she began hesitantly. "There's the hell of seeing something good go bad, the hell of being despised and disregarded, the hell of wrong paths. You can take a wrong path, casually, and have it end up being your life."

He didn't move a muscle. There was nothing to indicate the quickening of excitement he felt at her first tentative confidences. If she gave him the keys, maybe he could unlock the door.

She paused a moment, then said in a carefully expressionless voice, "There's the hell of wishing someone dead and getting your wish." Jesse sucked in a breath in sympathy with the pain she must have felt.

Abruptly she sat up and swung her legs off the bed. He watched her walk to the window and look out, giving her a minute to herself before he pushed himself up to follow.

She felt his warmth behind her and turned her head to caress his shoulder with her cheek. Together they looked out the window. The mist had stretched itself thin. There were clear patches now between the wisps of fog.

"It wasn't your fault," he said. "You're not responsible for Brian's death."

"No?" she asked, really wondering, then she answered her own question. "No, I suppose not, but somehow it's all tangled up in my head. I felt tied to him, so I wished he was dead. He died, and I was free. I can't explain it. It's not clear and logical, but you can't imagine how many times I've wished I'd left him. Then, if he'd died . . . Oh, I know it doesn't make sense."

It didn't, Jesse agreed to himself, and yet it did.

"And maybe," she added, "if I'd left him he wouldn't have had to carouse quite so defiantly. You see, I knew a part of his roistering was guilt. He wasn't bad, just spoiled and childish. He didn't love me, but he did like me."

Jesse rubbed her shoulders in silent sympathy. He wasn't sure there was anything else he could do for her. No matter what he said, she still had to think it through herself.

She leaned back against him. "Do you think I was weak to stay with Brian?" she asked. "My mother always said I was a born martyr."

Jesse's mouth quirked. It sounded like the kind of remark *his* mother might make. He thought before answering. "A lot of people think it's weak to put yourself second. When the one in first place is a child, I don't agree." He was telling her he knew she'd stayed for Tad.

She closed her eyes, feeling an absurd urge to cry. How many times had she wanted to hear someone say all the things he was saying? She turned suddenly, swaying toward him, then stopped herself. "I was going to throw my arms around you," she said, smiling tremulously, "but I can't."

"Save that impulse," he commanded. Then he drew her close. "You know, Betsy, I have this awful feeling I'm about a year too early. You'll work your way out of all this, I know you will. But until then, I'm the trigger for a whole lot of old pain. See me, and you see the past. Maybe we *should* have made a date for a year or two from now. I'm pushing you, and I know it's hard for you."

She bit her lip. "If I could just separate you from football . . ." She couldn't deny anything he'd said.

"But you can't. I'm associated with the lifestyle and with your past." His voice held a bleakness that made her want to explain her feelings further. Her forehead furrowed with the effort.

"I've tried to figure out why I hate football so much. I think what I was most afraid of the first three years of Tad's life was being tied to Brian forever." She went on. "I knew, even then, that I couldn't stay with him much longer, even for Tad. But if he'd been badly hurt, I'd have had to."

Jesse smiled. To her that was a given. It would never occur to her that most people would leave instead of dig in at that point.

She laughed in self-denigration. "There's nothing selfless about my fear of football. I used to be terrified watching Brian play, and by now it's a reflex. I can't watch a game without fear, and I get the shudders when I think about Tad playing. I've tried not to be overprotective, but . . ." Her tone grew angry. "And now I have to worry about you too." She lifted her head to stare at him belligerently.

He looked at her thoughtfully. "That first game, with the Rangers, you looked worried. I wished it was for me."

She glanced down and away. He could hardly hear her low-voiced admission. "It was."

He lifted her chin with his finger. Looking into her eyes, he said, "Careful, lady. It's beginning to sound like maybe you like me."

She stared back at him. He was asking for an admission she wasn't prepared to make.

"Why don't you shut up and kiss me?" she demanded defiantly.

He laughed, then obliged.

Ten

Betsy awoke early the next morning and lay listening to the birds twittering in the live oaks outside the window. She was enjoying the freshness of the morning air and the feel of Jesse's shoulder under her head. He slept soundly, his chest rising and falling evenly. She resisted the urge to touch the golden stubble on his chin and cheeks.

When his eyelids fluttered, she experienced a sudden clutch of panic in her midsection, which alerted her to the fact that she wasn't as casual about their affair as she might like. How was she going to face him? she wondered. What did last night mean? Were they lovers from now on? Panicky thoughts spiraled through her brain. She hadn't had any practice at this. What were you supposed to say in the bright light of day to a man who knew all your nighttime secrets?

She tried to imagine sipping coffee and reading the morning newspaper with Jesse on the other side of the breakfast table, but she failed. If he were on the other side, she wouldn't be able to concentrate on the paper. She suddenly felt she needed to be away when he woke up. She slid slowly from beneath his forearm and tiptoed to the shower.

She was dressed in linen slacks and shirt and was

brushing her hair when Jesse woke up. In the dressing-table mirror she saw him groping for her with his eyes closed. She stifled a giggle.

Encountering empty sheets, he hoisted himself to a sitting position and groaned. In the mirror, she saw him find her. Warmth spread through her chest at the way his face lit. Without preamble, he said, "Come back to bed."

"And waste my five minutes of careful grooming?" she asked in mock indignation.

He grinned at her, looking so happy she found herself grinning back at his reflection in the mirror. A couple of loonies they were, she told herself. And this wasn't so hard. She still felt a little shy, but no paralysis. She stood and walked to the bed to kiss him.

"Mmmm," he murmured beneath her lips. His hand cupped her head to prolong the contact. His mouth had a slightly acrid taste, and his stubble prickled. Her heart began to pound. Night and day weren't very different after all, she discovered. One could shade into the other easily. She pulled away, breathless and flushed.

"You taste like toothpaste," he said. "Something minty. What's your brand?"

She giggled. "A practical man. You're supposed to pretend it's my lips that are ambrosial."

He lay back down, pulling her arm to take her with him. She put a hand on the bed to keep her weight off his injury. It looked worse in daylight, purple and black and yellow. Her expression grew concerned and she touched his ribs lightly. "Take care of this today, won't you? Shouldn't you be having therapy or something?"

"I had therapy last night."

He wasn't interested in the bruise. His gaze was roaming her face, and he had that bedroom look in his eyes. Her own eyes widened warily as he took up where he'd left off the night before.

"Jesse . . ." she gasped as his busy mouth moved to her throat.

"Mmmm?" His fingers were working at her top button. Her hand closed over them before he could make much progress.

"Stop!" she commanded, laughing. "I have to go."

He blew out a frustrated breath and dropped his head back onto the pillow. "Damn," he said quietly, smiling intimately at her.

She smiled back, feeling a little shy. He read the hesitancy in her face. "Why do I get the feeling you were going to sneak out of here?" His expression was wise and amused.

Haughtily she said, "I was just trying to relieve you of an embarrassing situation. The morning-after syndrome?"

He shook his head. "Uh-uh. Wrong fella. I've never been embarrassed in my life."

She believed that. Audacity was his middle name.

"Don't be embarrassed, Betsy, ever. There's no need. It's not like that between us. There'll never be a time when I don't want to see you."

She looked at him doubtfully. That she didn't believe, but it was good to hear the words. "Okay," she said to end the discussion. She added a quick kiss and gave him a flashing smile before shoving herself up.

He watched her walk briskly to the dressing table, recognizing some remnant of her old urge to run. Give it time, he counseled himself. She'd come a long way to meet him. She wasn't as ready as he was to settle in.

"Where are you going?" he asked matter-of-factly.

She turned with the hairbrush raised to repair the damage to her hair. "I'm here for a course, remember?" she said, then added tartly, "Even if it was your reputation instead of mine that got me the invitation." In the mirror she could see the sheepish look on his face. She raised her eyebrows. "Ah, you thought I hadn't realized that?" She wrinkled her nose charmingly. "If you weren't such a good lover, you'd hear more about it."

He smiled at her, leaning back with his arms folded behind his head. The bruise looked terrible, but he was moving more easily today, she noted. One knee was propped in the air. He looked like a statue of an arrogant Hercules, completely unself-conscious.

She scooped up her purse and notebook and headed for the door. " 'Bye," she caroled. He watched her go, then lay back down on the bed after the door closed behind her. Damn, he felt good.

Unexpectedly, the door reopened and Betsy's head poked around it. "This probably won't interest you, as you're never embarrassed," she said guilelessly, "but the maid's finished next door, and this room's next."

The noise of an approaching vacuum cleaner emphasized her words. Jesse yelped, dragging the sheet across himself. Betsy closed the door. He heard her laugh receding down the hall.

Jesse spent the morning with Fred Hoff, inspecting some new casks of Hungarian oak the vintner was experimenting with. When they finally emerged from the aging cellars, the sun had dissipated the morning mists. It was unseasonably hot.

Heading back to the house, they saw Betsy coming toward them, carrying a picnic basket. She'd changed to a full flowered skirt, and the wind blew it around her calves. To Jesse she looked like spring and summer. He quickened his steps, getting to her in time to relieve her of the basket before Fred caught up with them.

"Hi," he said, his voice deep and intimate. "I've missed you." His thumb stroked her lower lip, which was still swollen from last night's attentions.

Gentle, slumbrous eyes smiled into his. "I've missed you too. I couldn't concentrate on the seminar. I'm glad it ended early. We're going on a picnic." She touched her tongue to his thumb, drawing a quick breath from him.

"Clever girl." His gaze approved everything about her. She basked in his warmth.

Fred greeted her.

"Hello," she replied. "I hope you don't mind. I talked your chef into letting me pack a meal. I thought I'd steal Jesse for a while if you can spare him."

Fred recognized romance when he saw it. He chuckled and waved assent. "Of course, of course. I've monopolized him all morning. Enjoy yourselves."

They strode up the hill hand in hand, pausing every few steps to gaze and smile at each other. Once Jesse said, "Do you think it would be too obvious if we went to your room for lunch?"

"Maybe a little obvious," she said regretfully. "A siesta, now, we might get away with that."

They passed through thickets of oak and terraced vineyards resting in red and gold splendor after a productive season. Jesse stepped aside for a word with one of the seasonal workers, who was carrying a forty-pound lug of grapes to the waiting gondolas. It was the last of the harvest. Soon all the activity would be centered in the fermenting vats, the bottling rooms, and the aging cellars.

"The harvest is the most exciting time up here," Jesse told Betsy, taking her hand again and pulling her up a steep bit of the path onto a knoll. "The whole valley hums. The locals are all on edge waiting to see if it's a good vintage or not."

She looked at him curiously. How odd that she should know every plane of his face and not know how he spent his free time. "Do you come up here often? You seem to know a lot about wines."

"I come every chance I get." He set the basket on the ground and took both her hands in his, needing to touch her. "I'd like to retire here someday. In fact, there's a place coming on the market that I've got my eye on. I'll show it to you on the way home. You'll ride back with me, won't you?"

She flashed him a grin. "Anything to escape the Inquisition. Torquemada had nothing on Vernon Curtin."

"Will you get the job?" He dropped her hands and stooped to spread the tablecloth he found on top of the basket.

"If I don't, I'm going to present him with a bill for consulting services."

She unpacked the food while Jesse stretched out on the grass and watched, wanting her again and knowing he would soon have her. He could wait. He enjoyed the ordinariness of hearing her hum while she worked. Her gaze rested on him as often as on the food. Finally she sat back on her heels, hands on hips, while she checked to make sure everything was ready.

"There," she pronounced in satisfaction. "A feast."

He smiled. "You're so damn cute."

She blushed at the look in his eyes, laughing in pleasure and surprise.

"And I'm so glad you still blush," he added with teasing satisfaction.

She stuck out her tongue. "I don't. Haven't in years. It has something to do with you. Behave, now, and eat."

He closed one eye to squint dubiously at the marinated prawns and ratatouille. "No ham sandwiches?" he asked without hope, then laughed at Betsy's indignant expression .

"I don't think we're compatible," she said threateningly.

He rose to a sitting position and reached for a prawn. As he held it to her lips, her mouth suddenly went dry. She obediently took a bite, but her thoughts were not all on the food.

After lunch they were lazy. Jesse lay on his back watching the sky. Bees hummed and insects clicked in the grass. He wondered what Betsy would look like naked in the sunshine. His eyes closed on a wave of yearning. Soon. It would have to be soon.

Betsy stretched out beside him. She picked a blade of grass and drew it across his throat. He smiled with his eyes still closed. She smiled, too, memorizing every detail of his face for the future. Nostalgia must have been invented when summer was changing to autumn, she decided. She sighed, feeling nostalgic for this day already.

"I'll bet you were an adorable kid," Jesse said, looking up at her. She wore no makeup, and he thought he could see a freckle or two popping out on her sun-kissed face.

She laughed. "I wasn't. I was hopeless. Too tall, too thin, and awkward as the dickens. My maiden name was Clark, and they used to call me B.C., because I was so backward socially. Brian called me that sometimes, too, because Carmody still fit."

Jesse's lips tightened. He didn't think that was amusing.

She looked down at him. "Did you have a nickname?"

"At least a dozen. The most popular ones were Bandit and Outlaw. My middle name's James."

She grinned, thinking those nicknames were appropriate.

"Don't say it," he warned, looking up at her through narrowed eyes. She resisted. After a moment he complained, "I'm cooking."

"Braised beef," she murmured.

"There you go again, focusing on the wrong appetite."

She lay on her side with her head propped on one hand, thinking how gorgeous he was. "Not altogether," she said softly.

His eyes opened wide. "Miz Carmody," he drawled, rolling over to face her, "I do believe that was a suggestive remark."

Lying side by side and looking into each other's eyes, they took turns unfastening buttons and zippers. They hadn't touched or kissed yet, but both of them were breathing hard.

"Will anyone come?" Betsy whispered.

"Not here," Jesse promised. "I paid one of the pickers to warn off any wanderers."

"Schemer." She groaned as his mouth found one of her breasts.

She fell onto her back, trembling and melting, instantly ready for him.

His voice shook as he said, "You're more beautiful in sunlight than by candlelight. Someday I'm going to spend five hours just making love to your lips and breasts."

She held out her arms, smiling, and agreed. "Someday. Not now."

When he tried to roll over her, she resisted, murmuring, "No. Your doctor would want you on your back. I could get sued if you have a relapse."

She rose to straddle his body, watching his eyes follow her as if he were his first sight of heaven, then watching them close as together they moved a little closer to their own personal paradise.

Afterward, lying on the crook of his arm, Betsy said, "That fight between you and Brian. It was he who called me a wet blanket, not you." Her voice held a quiet certainty.

Jesse went very still. "He told you I said that?" he asked carefully.

She nodded against his arm. "But you didn't."

More interested in the answer to his next question than in the past, he asked expressionlessly, "How do you know?"

"I just do."

There was silence except for the birds and insects and Jesse's breathing, which was as loud as if he'd been running. Slowly Betsy turned to look at him. She forced herself not to flinch from the tense joy in his eyes. They looked at each other for minutes, till Betsy felt herself trembling from the effort not to pull away.

Finally Jesse dropped his head onto the ground with a sigh and pressed Betsy's face close into his shoulder. It was a beginning, he told himself. A strong beginning. But they both knew how fragile this early intimacy was. He felt like a man walking on eggshells, not an easy task when you weigh two hundred and twenty-five pounds.

The sun was setting and fog was rolling over the Marin hills as they drove across the Golden Gate Bridge into the city.

"Tad's with Olivia?" Jesse asked.

"Yes. Or rather, Olivia's with Tad. There's more room at my place, so she and Alex slept there. Tad was supposed to go to the Tanners for a while today. He probably didn't miss me at all." She smiled, relaxed and happy as a well-fed cat.

Jesse reached for her hand. He wished the weekend didn't have to end. He had a feeling it was too good to last.

When Betsy opened her front door and called, "Anybody home?" Tad's small body caromed down the hall, and he hurled himself at her. "Mom! You're back!" He wore a gauze bandage above one eye.

"Tad! What did you do to your head?"

He'd spotted Jesse behind her. "Jesse!" he exclaimed joyfully, abandoning his mother without a qualm. "Guess what I did today!"

"What?" Jesse tossed him into the air by way of a greeting.

Betsy wanted an answer. "Tad, your head. What happened?"

Impatiently, he said, "It's nothing, Mom. I got a cut." He continued animatedly to Jesse, "I threw two touchdown passes. Me and Blaine beat Hap and Skippy in the park."

"No kidding!" Jesse was suitably impressed.

Betsy's hands went to her hips. "Tad, I need an explanation. How did you cut your head?" Her voice was rising.

Over his shoulder he said, "Playing football, Mom. I fell down. It's okay." Evidently feeling that Jesse was more in tune with the day's accomplishments than his mother, he turned back to him. "I got three stitches at the 'mergency room." His eyes were wide with self-importance. "And I didn't even cry."

His eyes brimming with humor at Tad's acquisition of macho values, Jesse glanced at Betsy. But Betsy was not amused. The laughter faded from Jesse's face as he saw that she was really upset.

"Let your mother have a look at your wounds, son," he told the boy gently.

That was a mistake. Something inside Betsy was shrieking, *Don't call him son. He's not your son. He'll only get hurt if he starts to think he is.*

She stared frozenly at Jesse as the boy obediently trotted to her.

Jesse's forehead furrowed. He'd known it was too good to last, but he hadn't expected it to blow up in his face so soon. His jaw clenched, and the puzzled look changed to a frown. So be it, he decided. He had never run from a fight in his life.

Betsy tried to loosen the bandage to see the cut beneath.

"Ow, Mom!" Tad pulled away. "That hurts. It's okay, really, the doctor said so. I might not even have much of a scar." Betsy's jaw dropped. If that was supposed to be reassuring . . . !

"I need to see it," she insisted, reaching for him. "Are you supposed to have it checked? How did you fall down? Were you tackled?"

Tad squirmed under the barrage of questions, and Jesse frowned in sympathy. The time for coddling was when the accident had just happened. Betsy's anxiety was only upsetting the boy now.

"He's all right, Betsy. Let him be," he said against his better judgment. She looked at him as if she didn't know him, but she was quiet.

Olivia bustled in from the kitchen. "Hi! Did you have a good time? Oh, hello, Jesse. You went too?" She looked from one to the other of them, registering the tensions. "Sandra said she'd call later to tell you about the cut. She feels terrible, of course." She ruffled Tad's hair. "But this young man survived it. I think he enjoyed the trip to the doctor as much as the visit to Blaine's."

Tad grinned sheepishly. Jesse smiled at Olivia, grateful for the perspective she was providing.

Betsy was still frozen, though. She knew she should loosen up, but she was afraid her lips would tremble if she relinquished control of her emotions. She was being silly, but she couldn't help herself. She laughed jerkily. "Well, it was an eventful weekend." She avoided Jesse's eyes. "Where's Alex, Liv?"

Olivia made a wry face. "I sent him home. He left his homework there, thinking he'd get out of doing it." She glanced at her watch. "But I'd better get back and check on him. He needs an armed guard, not a mother."

Betsy followed her to the kitchen, thanking her and exchanging news.

Jesse squatted down to talk to Tad. "Want some help getting ready for bed?" he asked. "You can tell me about the game."

Tad nodded eagerly.

Betsy saw Olivia off and climbed the stairs slowly. Tad was in his pajamas and in bed, leaning toward Jesse trustingly.

Jesse smiled at her and got off the bed, saying, " 'Night, Tad. Your mom'll tuck you in." He studied Betsy's pale face as he passed her in the doorway. "Tad's teeth are brushed. I'll wait for you downstairs."

She nodded, struggling with renewed resentment. What was the matter with her? She should be grateful that he'd gotten Tad ready for bed. But she wasn't. She felt robbed of her special time with Tad after being away. Was she selfish? she asked herself. She'd been number one with Tad for so long. Had she come to need his dependence?

That wasn't all that was bothering her, though. At the pit of her stomach was an icy fear that came from seeing how much Jesse already meant to Tad. What was she letting him in for? What was she letting herself in for?

It was an affair she'd agreed to. Okay, he'd forced her to admit she was a woman and she needed a man. But it didn't have to mean more, did it? The last time she took a lover, she'd found herself married to a spoiled child. From here on out, *she* controlled her life. She'd better make that clear to Jesse before he took over.

"Want a bedtime story, Tadpole?" she asked gently.

Tad smiled and held out his arms. She sat on the bed and hugged him, feeling tears spring to her eyes. He had missed her. He hadn't even protested when she'd called him Tadpole.

Jesse was sitting on the couch reading the newspaper and sipping a glass of brandy.

"Can I offer you a glass of your brandy?"

She nodded. "Thanks." She wandered over to an easy chair and sat down, wanting to avoid an invitation to share the couch just now. He handed her a glass and sat back down while she took a sip.

"You're upset about Tad's cut." He was stating the obvious. She nodded, staring at nothing.

"Is it because he got hurt playing football?"

Her mouth twisted. "Probably. It's such a brutal game."

"It's life, Betsy," Jesse insisted. "We're a warrior species."

Strange, she thought. She'd always visualized football players as warriors too. That's what it was out there, a war.

"We started out that way," she argued, looking at him. "I'd like to think we've evolved some since then."

He shrugged. "I'd like to think so, too, but the evidence is against us. Testing yourself by hunting or fighting has always been a masculine thing."

"It's just too risky, and the risk of Tad's playing football increases with his exposure to football players."

Jesse shook his head, bewildered. "Betsy! The freeway's risky. So's breathing, these days. So's sitting at a desk for thirty years and getting heart disease."

She rubbed her forehead. She could feel a migraine coming on.

"Headache?" he asked sympathetically.

She nodded. "Would you mind if I just said good night, Jesse?"

He placed his glass on the coffee table. "No. I should get home too." Standing up, he added, "Will I see you tomorrow?"

She shook her head. "Not tomorrow. I have a catering job." She pulled herself to her feet. The headache was getting worse by the minute.

"When, then?" Jesse demanded, his face stern. He knew what was happening.

She rubbed her forehead again, distractedly. "I don't know. I'll call you."

"I'd like to take Tad sailing one evening this week."

She looked him in the eye. "Let's leave it for now, shall we? He's had a big weekend. I'd like him to have a few ordinary days. I wouldn't want him to start expecting a full-time diet of excitement."

He nodded in confirmation. Somehow he'd thought she'd say that. He realized she was really going to deny what had happened between them. Man, he'd had some rejections in his life, but nothing to match this.

He almost said, "Sure. Call me next time you want a little fling," but when she raised her hand to her eyes again, he knew she was hurting too. She was fighting her own demons. He drew in a deep breath and expelled it slowly. He'd fight them, too, but later. Right now he had to go somewhere to absorb the blow.

"Better take something for that headache."

She nodded. "I will."

He put his palm to her forehead in a fleeting gesture, then turned to go. "See you," he said grimly over his shoulder.

This time it was more a threat than a promise.

Eleven

Betsy stared at the measuring spoons in her hand, trying to remember whether or not she'd put the cream of tartar in the eggwhites. She sighed. These lapses had come all too often during the last two days.

Across the table Olivia hummed as she piped ladyfingers onto a parchment template. Betsy wondered glumly how she could be so happy.

She put the spoons down and wandered over to her desk. The little red light gleamed on the answering machine. For a minute she stared at it, afraid to play the messages back. She'd told Jesse she'd call him, and she hadn't. Would his angry voice be on the tape?

She was aching to talk to him. More than once she'd picked up the phone to call him, but every time the unanswered questions in her mind made her replace the receiver before she dialed. What would she say to him? "I miss you, stay away from my son"?

She should have thought it through before she'd let things go so far. She'd known all along Jesse wouldn't settle for a tidy, discreet affair. He'd bulldoze his way into her life, and it would never be the same. She'd see her picture in gossip columns. It could even affect her business.

She couldn't avoid the issue forever. Firming her

lips, she flipped the switch. The tape whirred as it rewound. She hit 'replay' and heard a tinny version of Jesse's voice say with frustration, "Okay, it was an interesting exercise in patience. Now I want to hear from you."

The next two messages were from Jesse too. The second was a list of three phone numbers where he could be reached. The third and loudest message was, "Dammit, Betsy, you said you'd call!"

An image of him popped into her mind, sunlight highlighting his hair and his neck muscles corded as he threw his head back to laugh. She blew out another deep breath as she reset the answering machine.

Olivia looked up from her ladyfingers. "For Pete's sake call the man," she said with violent irritation. "You're driving me nuts with these moody sighs!"

Betsy made a face at her. "What would one do without the sweet support of one's friends?"

Olivia snorted. "You need a swift supporting kick to the—"

Betsy blocked the rest with hands over her ears. "Stop! I'm getting enough arguments from myself. I don't need one from you."

"You've got what most women would give their legs for, and you're mucking around with it." Olivia squirted batter with more force than necessary. "What *is* it you're afraid of?"

"Tad losing another father figure, to begin with," Betsy replied promptly.

Always professional, Olivia finished the ladyfingers before she put her hands on her hips and glared at Betsy. "Tad's human," she said, "so, yes, he might get hurt occasionally."

Betsy glared back. "He's been hurt enough!"

"I can't see any signs of lasting damage in *him*," Olivia said meaningfully. "How long are you going to use Tad as an excuse to avoid life?" At the stricken look on Betsy's face Olivia dropped her hands and her belligerent tone and rounded the table to hug her friend.

"My evil tongue," she apologized. "I know you worry about Tad. You need to worry about yourself."

"I am!" Betsy said emphatically.

"Not the way I mean. Worry about getting what you need, not about being safe forever."

Betsy said in anguish, "I need Jesse, but I also need stability for Tad, self-respect, and peace. I can't see how to put them together. If I don't figure it out, I could lose everything."

"Let Jesse help you figure it out."

"That's just what I don't want—Jesse running my life!"

Olivia sighed. "Don't you trust him at all?"

"Of course I do. It's just . . ." She stopped. Shoulders sagging, she amended her last remark. "Maybe I don't, altogether." She nibbled on a thumbnail, frowning at her thoughts, then shrugged impatiently. "I'll call him in a little while, but right now I don't know what to say."

Olivia patted Betsy on the back. "Start with 'I'm nuts about you' and go from there," she said crisply.

Betsy laughed. "Sounds good. Maybe you're right."

She reached him at his apartment.

"Hi," she said.

"Well, hi," he replied in a sarcastic drawl. "Nice of you to call."

She bit her lip. He was going to be difficult. Of course, wasn't he always? "How are you, Jesse?"

"Fine." He couldn't have been more curt.

She sighed internally. "I mean really. How's your chest?"

"Is that the only reason you phoned, to inquire about my health?"

"No," she said indignantly.

"What, then?"

She drew an offended breath. What had she done to deserve this? "Well, why did *you* call *me*?" she demanded.

"Because I want to see you."

"Well, I want to see you, too," she countered angrily.

He laughed. "Are we having a lovers' quarrel?" he asked in a different tone.

She softened immediately. "I think we are. Is it over?"

"It's over. When can I see you?"

She thought quickly. "Tonight? Tad's going to Olivia's, so I could come to your place."

Across the table Olivia had her hands on her hips, and was shaking her head. Betsy shot her a pleading look. There was a silence on the line. Then Jesse said slowly, "I'll come there."

Too quickly she said, "Please, let's meet at your place. You don't have to clean house," she added, with fake coyness.

Jesse instinctively knew this was Betsy's way of holding him off. He could have her body, but he should stay out of her daily life. In a smooth, unyielding voice, he said, "Your place is homier. We can make a fire, put our feet up, settle in."

It sounded good enough to terrify her. She grimaced. "Okay. Will you be here for dinner?"

"Don't cook for me. I'll pick up some Chinese takeout on the way over."

She sighed and smiled. No help for it, she might as well enjoy herself. "All right, Jesse," she said softly, allowing herself to be loving for the first time that day. "See you later."

"With bells on," he promised warmly.

Olivia pounced when Betsy hung up the phone, ignoring the appeal on her friend's face. "Uh-uh! I'm not taking Tad, so that you can keep him and Jesse apart."

"Please, Liv, just this once. I wasn't going to ask you, but I already told Jesse Tad wouldn't be here. Besides," she added, switching tactics, "how can Jesse and I work things out with Tad underfoot?"

Olivia released an exasperated breath. "Oh, all right! I'll keep Tad, but you'd better have the time of your life."

Betsy smiled dazzlingly. "I will," she said, feeling weak at the knees just thinking about it.

● ● ●

Betsy lay half over Jesse on the living-room floor in front of the empty fireplace. There'd been no time to make a fire. They'd exchanged hellos, put the cartons of Chinese food in the kitchen, and fallen on each other as if they were starving, throwing clothes all over the room.

"Replete," Betsy murmured. "I think that's the word."

Jesse chuckled. "Are you cold?" he asked.

"Are you kidding? How about you? Do you want a fire?"

Another chuckle. "I think we had one. Do you suppose we'll ever get around to foreplay?"

"Jesse!" She'd never get used to his frankness about things sexual. It was more than frankness, actually. He used words in lovemaking as skillfully as he used his hands. And he used his hands very skillfully indeed.

He opened an eye when she rose to her knees. "I love the way you move, but where are you going?"

She regarded him teasingly. "To get my veils. I thought I'd dance for you."

She skipped out of reach with a giggle as he grabbed for her. "You don't need veils, come back here."

"Patience, patience," she scolded gently, gliding out of the room.

It was contagious, the ease Jesse had with his body, she thought. She felt no self-consciousness about her lack of clothes. Jesse's open appreciation of her body was thrilling to her, and the freedom to touch him any time she wanted to was a never-ending joy. She was discovering that her sexual appetite was stronger than she'd ever suspected.

She returned with utensils, plates, and the white cartons Jesse had brought with him. "Food for the inner man." Settling herself on her knees at the coffee table, she dished out the meal. "We should eat this way all the time. No spots on your tie."

He sat up, smiling, and moved to sit cross-legged beside her. "There are other advantages," he said, his gaze running over her from head to toe. With her tumbled hair and graceful, creamy-skinned limbs against the richness of an Oriental rug, she looked like a perfect subject for a Renoir painting. "You're quite a woman."

She looked at him and said seriously, "You're quite a man!"

He paused with his spoon in the kung pao chicken and glanced quickly at her. She held his gaze steadily. Whatever doubts she had about the clashing of their lifestyles, she had none about her feelings for him. "Starting to like me a bit?" he asked teasingly.

"A bit."

He dropped the spoon and reached for her hand. "Who needs food?"

She laughed, kissed him sweetly and swiftly, then said, "Later. Dish me up some of that chicken."

He shook his head while he scooped. "You lack romance, you know," he said sadly. She grinned and reached for the rice.

After eating they built a fire and piled up cushions in front of it. Jesse stretched his length against them and wrapped his arms around Betsy so that they both faced the flames. "When do I see you again?" he asked.

Betsy wasn't ready to face the real world. She turned in his arms and smiled seductively up at him. "It's later, now. Are you sure you want to talk?"

He grinned and looked down at her glowing face. He was tempted, but he recognized the evasion. "It'll still be later, later. Can I take you and Tad sailing tomorrow evening?"

"It's open house at Tad's school. He wants to show me around his classroom," she said apologetically.

Flames crackled to split the silence as Jesse waited to see if she'd invite him to come along. Instead she said, "How about the next night, after Tad's gone to bed?"

"I'm scheduled to work in the emergency room that night."

"Oh. How about this weekend?" she asked meekly.

"They say I'll be ready to play in Houston this weekend. And in Chicago next weekend."

"Oh." She should have realized that. His bruise looked better tonight. "Can you throw without pain?"

"More or less."

She discovered that she wasn't as happy about that as she should have been. It meant he'd be playing again. At least when he was convalescing he couldn't get hurt. "See you when you get back from Houston, then?"

"Yeah, probably," he said slowly. "Or maybe—how about Friday? I'm scheduled for the ER that night, too, but I think I could switch with someone."

Betsy was more enthusiastic. "That might work. Tad's having supper and spending the night at the Tanners' on Friday, but I'll be here."

It didn't escape Jesse that not one of her suggestions included Tad. And he didn't think it was because she wanted him all to herself. His voice was low. "I'll come when I get out of practice. I might drop in at Hap's on the way over. Any objection if I speak to Tad?" He couldn't keep the bitterness out of his tone.

"Jesse," she protested, "of course not." Pain and confusion tore through her. She hadn't meant to hurt him. She'd intended to steer the relationship subtly so that she could see Jesse and protect Tad. She should have known it wouldn't work. Jesse was too smart.

He let out a long, frustrated breath and stared over her head at the fire. In anguish she watched firelight bring the unhappy expression on his face into relief.

"Just tell me one thing, Betsy. Did it mean anything to you, the weekend in Napa?"

"Oh, Jesse, you know it did. Why would you doubt it?"

He gave a humorless laugh but was too dispirited to pursue the subject just then. "No reason." He lay still, concentrating on keeping his breathing even. He couldn't follow his inclinations and start yelling, or he'd blow the whole thing sky-high.

Betsy nibbled unhappily on her bottom lip. If there was to be any honesty between them at all, she thought, she had to tell him some of what she was feeling. He knew it, anyway. Softly she said, "I just need a little time to sort things out, Jesse. I want to be with you, but I'm afraid. Of so many things."

He drew in and released a slow, heavy breath. "We need to talk. Soon."

"Soon. We'll talk."

"I love you, Betsy," he said firmly.

Her eyes squeezed shut. "Oh, Jesse."

It was pain as much as love that moved him when he lowered her to the carpet. "Show me what the weekend meant to you, Betsy." His voice was low and rough. "I need you now."

She lifted her hands to draw his head down to her. Remorse and tenderness gave her lips and fingertips a new sensitivity. She stroked his face lightly, reading the creases in his forehead and the tension in his neck. She sighed into his mouth. She didn't want to put lines in his face, she wanted to make him smile.

With a new determination she moved her mouth against his and soothed his lips with her tongue. She couldn't eliminate her reservations about their relationship, but she could erase the lines from his forehead.

She slid her fingers to his shoulders and pressed. "I want to feel your weight on me," she whispered. He lowered himself, oh, so carefully, until her breasts flattened under him. She shuddered in satisfaction at the feel of his bulk and warmth. They were both breathing faster now. She slid her hands up and down the corded muscles of his back.

Excitement pulsated between them with each thunderous heart-surge of blood. Betsy was completely aroused and so, she knew, was Jesse, but they kept their movements deliberate. Both of them were stepping carefully, avoiding more bruises than just the one on Jesse's chest. This time, they'd go slowly. Who knew how long it would have to last?

• • •

The Monday night following the Chicago game, Jesse made his way down the side path of Betsy's house. She'd had enough time to think, he told himself. He'd given her breathing room, been her lover, let her distract him with her body from the issues between them. They'd had a honeymoon's worth of nights saturated with sexuality. Now he had a few things to say.

He looked at his watch. It was after ten. He'd hoped to see Tad too. But the coach had kept the team late to watch films of the game, which hadn't been one of their best efforts. They still had a chance to win their division title, but they'd have to beat the Centurions next week. He hoped they could do it. If they had to go into the play-offs as a wild card team, there'd be an extra game, and he could use a week off for healing.

From then on out the season would be grueling. He could look forward to bad weather on the road, extra hours studying plays and films, and tougher games played with or without injuries.

Betsy would be in the kitchen, working, he thought. He stepped onto the back deck and discovered he was right. The room was dim. Betsy, with her back to him, was bent over a small desk in a pool of light, taking notes from a thick book.

His palms grew damp at the sight of her. The lamplight drew red highlights from her hair. A wing of hair she'd tucked behind her ear swung forward onto her cheek, and she pushed it back with her thin, graceful hand.

He slid open the well-lubricated door and walked into the room. Over Betsy's shoulder he saw colored pictures of elaborate desserts.

"How do you stay so thin," he asked, "looking at all that stuff?"

She whirled and gasped, then her hand went to her heart as she sagged in relief. "Don't scare me like that!" she scolded.

He grinned. "You were deep in contemplation of your favorite natural beauties."

She rose and came to place her hands on his shoulders. After a lingering kiss of greeting she said gently, "I'm going to have a lock put on that gate."

"You should. You never know who might come wandering in here." He leaned against the high butcher-block table and pulled her against him, smiling with pleasure at the sight of her face.

He looked tired, she thought. She touched her knuckles to his cheekbone. "Rough game, huh?"

He shrugged it off. "I've had better. Why aren't you in bed on satin sheets, as befits the glamorous lady I saw on that television talk show Saturday?"

Her mouth twisted wryly. "Glamour has a high price." She was tired too.

"Workload getting you down?" he asked sympathetically.

She nodded, wondering why no one but Jesse made her feel like complaining and why she always felt so much better after she'd done it. "Someday," she said, "I'd like to have enough of a reputation to be able to drop all the public-relations stuff and just concentrate on writing and teaching."

"Why not now?" he asked, curious.

"Can't afford it."

He knew better than to offer to invest in her business, though the thought had crossed his mind. Instead, he grabbed her arms and swung her down like the best Hollywood sheik. With a maniacal gleam in his eyes, he said, "Let me take you away from all this. We'll live on McBurgers and ice cream. You'll never have to look at a *radicchio* again!"

Laughing, she said, "Jesse, you're crazy! Let me up."

He brought her upright, but kept her close, clasping his hands behind her waist and looking down at her in a way that brought heat to her cheeks. She stared back, and he changed his mind about holding back his offer to invest. He was tired of biting his tongue around her. He didn't want to see her beautiful face only on a weekly basis.

"You know," he said, "I'd really like to invest in your business so you could relax a bit and do what you want to right now." She opened her mouth to protest, and he held up his hand to stop her. "I'd also like to share some of the parenting load with you. I want more time with Tad. I'd like to be involved in your life. I don't want to be just a weekend stud."

She'd been concentrating more on how his face looked when he was serious, how his mouth moved, than on his words. He looked so good to her. She'd tossed and turned for three endless nights, now. She didn't want to spend this one arguing, but she knew it was inevitable.

While he was gone, she'd found photographers and reporters on her doorstep twice, and had endured a poisonous phone call from Jesse's ex-girlfriend, the actress Linda Ralston, who considered Betsy a poacher. She'd had a fight with Tad, who said life was boring when Jesse wasn't around, and she'd gotten a migraine from watching the game yesterday. Aside from their nights together, not much good was coming from their affair.

None of that changed the way she felt, though. Looking at his serious, intelligent face, she realized with wonder that she was in love with him. Beyond question and in spite of all reason, she loved him. She still didn't know how she could live her own life and love him, too, but she loved him.

A laugh bubbled from her chest. " 'Weekend stud,' " she echoed. "The things you say!"

Her provocative laugh stopped him in mid-thought. His smile grew slowly. She looked up at him through her thick lashes and moved her fingers to the top button of his shirt.

"We need to talk, lady," he said unconvincingly.

Her expression had a devilish quality he'd never seen in her before. His heart began to pound. As she reached the third button, he complained humorously, "You women are all alike, only interested in one thing. And when you've got it, 'Good-bye, Jesse.' " He was fooling, but there was a kernel of truth in what he said.

Betsy ignored him, concentrating on the unbutton-ing process. Blood roared in her ears. She felt as if everything in her was focused on Jesse and her love for him.

His face was flushed, his fists clenched. He watched her through narrowed eyes, his chest rising and falling heavily. "No talking, huh?"

She shook her head as she undid the last button and slipped her hands inside to find his flesh. Talking was far too dangerous. Sex was risky enough, but talk-ing, growing close, learning to need him—that was dangerous.

"Where's Tad?" he asked while he could still think of practical details.

"Upstairs asleep. It would take an earthquake to wake him."

"You're going to serve me up on the table, are you?" Jesse's voice wasn't quite steady.

Betsy was far too excited to walk down the hall and up the stairs.

She reached for his hand, shivering with her need for him. "I'll let you in on a little caterer's secret." She led him into a small room, hardly more than a closet, which was lined with racks of waiters' uniforms, shelves of serving dishes, and cans of various staple items. "In case of spills," she said, indicating the soft carpet on the floor.

A potent combination of excitement and anger had grown in Jesse until his recklessness matched hers. Betsy saw the muscles in his jaw clench before he reached behind her and pushed the door partially closed. The storeroom was lit only by a line of light from the kitchen. In the darkness there was no sound but their hoarse breathing.

He took her arms and dragged her to him. All the frustration of the last two weeks was poured into the kiss he branded onto her lips, and she reveled in the heat and pressure of it.

She whimpered when he pulled away. "I can't resist

you and you know it," he said. "You've been using it, but it won't work forever. I want this, but I want more." His fingers tangled in her hair. "Afterwards, we're going to talk. So you'll want to make this last, won't you?"

As she followed him to the carpet, she thought, *he knows too much. He always has.*

Twelve

"Where are they!" Betsy muttered through clenched teeth as she paced the house. She flooded the front rooms with light, trying to banish her fears with the shadows.

Against her better judgment she'd let Tad go with Alex to tonight's Miner-Centurion game, the last before the play-offs. Football loomed so large in Tad's mind right now that a refusal would have meant a major confrontation between them. They had already had one run-in this week when she wouldn't let him call Jesse.

"No, Tad," she'd said, realizing that her excuses were running thin. "He's preparing for the play-offs. We really shouldn't impose on him right now."

Tad wasn't buying it. "You just don't want me to see him! Why not? Am I ever going to have a dad?" He'd looked at her as if she were his enemy.

She closed her eyes to shut out the memory. Things had gone further than she'd thought. Tad loved Jesse. What was she going to do? Maybe Tad did have a right to his own relationships, even if they ended up hurting him. She couldn't protect him forever.

Just now that seemed like a minor worry. In her mind, images of Brian tangled in steel chased visions of buses plunging down cliffs. Tad and Alex were riding the bus. Was she out of her mind? Buses didn't have seat belts! If she had to let him go, why didn't she at least drive him? She'd watched the game anyway.

She did an about-face at the end of the hall, pacing back toward the door with her arms folded tightly across her chest. Her head was pounding, and she was seeing little spots before her eyes. Another migraine was coming on.

It had started during a pregame interview. The camera had showed Jesse laughing and waving good-bye to blond Janet Larson, a well-known local news anchor woman who'd so far resisted offers to star in films. Watching, Betsy had felt depression settle over her like a collapsed tent. That was her competition, she'd told herself—women who were so beautiful they made her feel like Whistler's grandmother.

Then there was the interview. Jesse was doing his colorful-personality act, white teeth flashing in a devilish grin that shot pangs of longing through her. "It won't be much of a game," he drawled. "More of a massacre. We're going to knock them out of the play-offs."

He was bluffing, of course. This was no lark for him. She could tell by the way he threw the ball during warm-ups that he was in pain.

It was a messy game. What had started as a light drizzle ended in a downpour. By the third quarter, Jesse was covered in mud. He slipped and slithered, trying to find solid enough footing to throw, and he took more than his share of hits. Betsy screamed out loud when one three-hundred-pound lineman hit him with a crushing tackle.

What were they doing out there? she asked herself. Jesse's ribs were taped, and Hap was playing with a broken finger. Probably a third of the team was hurt in some way by now.

They didn't even seem to notice. This game was crucial, and every man's face reflected it. There was an intensity in their play that Betsy hadn't seen before. In spite of herself she was drawn into the drama.

She wanted to see brutality and stupidity. She saw

pride, courage, and determination. Slogging through mud, being knocked to the ground, Jesse never wavered in his concentration on getting the ball into the end zone. He picked himself off the ground without a glance at his tacklers, his gaze following the ball. He wiped sweat and mud from his eyes and urged a teammate on with a slap on the back.

Where *were* they? Betsy's pacing picked up speed as fear generated fury in her. Alex was in for the lecture of his life. If he was going to be this late, he should at least call her!

She grabbed her coat. She'd go to the sidewalk, leaving the door open in case the phone rang. From the bottom of the steps she could see the bus stop. She opened the door and stared stupidly as Jesse's silver Jaguar pulled to a stop at the curb. Jesse's head appeared above the roof of the car.

"Have you seen Tad?" she called anxiously.

"Right here."

The passenger door opened and Tad's small figure appeared, wearing a battered Miners' helmet and a starry-eyed expression. Betsy's relief was swallowed in an anger so great it made her hands shake. She clenched them into fists and snapped her mouth shut with an audible click.

Tad waved and patted his head. "Mom, look what I got! Jesse said I can keep it!"

She couldn't answer. Whatever she said right now would scare him.

Jesse escorted Tad up the steps, his eyes narrowing at Betsy's rigid silence. "Bedtime, son," he said. "You can show your mom the helmet tomorrow." He ushered Tad past Betsy. "Can you get yourself in bed tonight, and fast?" he asked. "You're old enough for that, aren't you? I want to talk to your mom."

Tad nodded. He'd probably jump off Coit Tower if Jesse asked him, Betsy thought. Tad looked over his shoulder uncertainly. "G'night, Mom."

"Good night, sweetheart," she managed.

She and Jesse watched Tad bound up the stairs,

then both of them turned toward the living room. Jesse followed Betsy in and shut the door. "What gives?" he asked quietly. She was facing the windows, but her back was eloquent with fury.

"Where's Alex?" she asked. "He was supposed to bring Tad home."

"I was coming anyway, so I dropped Alex off at home. I didn't like the idea of Tad traveling on the bus at night."

"You should have called me." She kept her back to him. Her head was pounding and nausea was churning in her stomach. She was seeing through a white haze.

"I'm sorry if you were worried." He sounded grim, not sorry. Betsy had been keeping him and Tad apart with one excuse or another for weeks. He didn't feel apologetic.

"Did you have to give him the helmet?" she demanded, her voice so low he could hardly hear it.

Coach Paulson had given Tad the helmet, but it didn't matter. She'd hold him responsible. "Betsy, turn around," he said in exasperation. "I want to see your face."

When she pivoted slowly, he felt as if he were looking at a stranger. Gone was the sweetness, the sensitivity. Her face was dead white, and her eyes looked black. He almost cried out and stepped to take her in his arms, but her words stopped him.

"Don't give me orders," she said in a hostile tone.

A muscle twitched in his jaw. "I don't like talking to people's backs. Betsy, what's going on?"

"You have no right to take my son without my permission."

He studied her. "Were you frightened? Is that it?" He was struggling to find the reality in this bizarre scene. He walked toward her. Where was his Betsy? She was completely out of reach.

She held up an arresting hand. "Don't touch me."

His eyebrows contracted in a frown. "All right," he said slowly. He gestured toward the furniture. "Shall we sit down? We'll talk."

He'd become very formal and polite, but his eyes were starting to glow with an anger to match hers, Betsy noticed. Fine, she thought. Let him be angry. Her impulse was to refuse him any cooperation, to say, "I'll stand," but she felt that would sound childish. She moved stiffly to a chair and sat, clasping her hands to control their trembling.

"Look," he said, "I understand that you were worried, and I think I understand why. But Tad wasn't that much later than he would have been if he'd taken the bus, and I think he was safer with me. So there's something else going on here, right?"

"Maybe there is," she admitted.

"The helmet?"

"Partly." She was proud of herself for the reasonableness of her tone.

"But more. You don't want him spending time with me." She said nothing. "And it's not just because I play football." Again nothing.

"What then?" he demanded angrily.

His anger jolted her into response. "I don't want him hurt when you leave."

"I'm not going anywhere." It was a threat.

"You are, eventually."

"Only if you drive me away."

She stared over his shoulder, trying to think and coming up with nothing but memories. "You say he's a good kid," she said slowly. "But you don't know the struggle it's been to keep him that way."

He waited, leaning forward on the couch, his elbows resting on his knees.

"He was a nice child until he was three. Then Brian started coming home loaded with presents and undermining me in every way he could. Tad would be uncooperative and disrespectful for days afterward. He was growing up to be just like Brian."

A muscle twitched in Jesse's cheek. "He's like that when he's been with me?"

"He's not uncooperative, but he's wild and excitable."

"Could there be a difference between normal excitement and a generally bad influence?"

"I suppose so," she conceded reluctantly.

"Are you sure you're not just jealous?" Jesse asked.

She gasped and grew even paler, but the expression in her eyes told Jesse she was thinking about it.

"Maybe I am," she admitted at last, "and maybe I was jealous of Brian too. But that doesn't negate what I was saying. Tad has to have some stability in his life."

"And you're the only one who can provide that?" Jesse bit the words out.

Her chin went up. "So far, yes."

He shook his head, feeling angry and sad. "Betsy, Betsy," he said in frustration, "why can't you trust me?"

"I know you mean well, Jesse, but I just don't see it working for us. Your life is glamour and glitter: TV appearances, beautiful women, travel, money. I can't handle it. I don't want Tad exposed to it."

He looked at her with an expression close to dislike. "Don't you know anything about me after all this time?" If her head hadn't been pounding, she might have seen the hurt behind his anger.

"I knew Brian longer than I've known you, and it turned out I didn't know him at all."

He slapped the coffee table so hard, it sounded like a whip cracking. "I'm not Brian!" he said savagely. "How long am I going to go on paying for his sins?"

She jumped, frightened in spite of herself at the violence in his voice. All her life the sound of a roaring male voice had been able to reduce her to jelly. Her hold on rationality slipped. "Don't yell at me!" she said shrilly. "Who do you think you are?"

"I thought I was the man in your life," he snarled, nostrils flaring. "I guess I was wrong. I was only the man in your bed."

She flinched as if she'd been struck.

He was in too much pain to care if he hurt her. "I told you I didn't believe in hell. Well, I forgot about purgatory. That's where I've been these past weeks. Not a pleasant place."

He got to his feet. She stood also, feeling too vulnerable with him towering over her. She stared at the determination on his face like a mouse staring at a cobra.

"One thing," he said quietly and menacingly. "For the record, I know that you care for me. You're just too much of a coward to admit it."

His eyes were black and burning. She looked away and whimpered softly.

He didn't even hear her. "Stay in your cocoon if you like," he said fiercely. "Just ask yourself if it's fair to keep Tad there, too."

The nausea in her stomach rose to her throat. If he didn't go soon, she'd be sick. She struggled to speak. "Tad and I were happy before you came along," she said in a ragged whisper. "What makes you think you're indispensable? I might want to sleep with you, but I don't want you running my life."

The anger he'd displayed before was nothing compared to the fury she'd now brought forth. Here was the passion beneath the easy-going facade Jesse Kincaid presented to the world. He took her arms and shook her once, not hard, but strongly. Her gaze flew to his contorted face. Through gritted teeth, he said harshly, "Lie to yourself if you like, but don't lie to me! You're afraid to take a chance at happiness. That's all this is!"

Trembling all over, she said, "Get out of my house."

"I'm going," he said, inches from her face, "but before I do here's a little something to make it harder for you to lie to yourself."

His fingers gripped her arms as he kissed her. With his mouth on hers, Betsy felt a kernel of longing in the midst of her fear, and it frightened her more than anything to discover the hold he had on her senses.

He lifted his head, his breath whistling angrily through his nostrils. His face was pale beneath his tan. "Was that lust," he demanded, "or something else?"

She swayed, her hand flying up to her lips.

In disgust, and with a remorse he refused to admit,

Jesse said, "Ah, it was only fear. There's too much of that to leave room for anything else. My mistake."

He set her away from him with a gentleness that clashed oddly with what had just passed. Then he strode from the room.

She heard the front door open and close before her legs buckled. Kneeling on her elegant oriental carpet, she held herself up with stiff arms, breathing deeply to control the nausea.

Along with the sickness and shivering she felt a deep and terrible sense of bereavement.

Thirteen

Betsy stared across the table at Garrett's smooth, well-groomed face with a sense of irritation. He looked so clean. He sounded so self-satisfied. Once she had admired that. Now, she felt like reaching over and loosening his tie.

The light from the candle on their table at Bernie's Restaurant shone on his fine blond hair. "And then I said, 'J.B., I'm a stockbroker, not a magician.'" Garrett laughed, pleased with himself. "I think he liked that. He likes a man who can stand up to him." He beamed at Betsy, sure of her approval.

She smiled dutifully and tuned him out again, counting on body language to provide her with her next cue. How much longer could he drag this story out? she wondered. Garrett was never a thrilling companion, but she usually felt happy and relaxed with him. Tonight she just felt bored. She wondered if she could plead a headache and end the evening early. She did feel one building.

She'd had too many headaches lately. One a day, at least. She tried to tell herself it was a message that she couldn't afford any more episodes like the one with Jesse. Her life was too full to add extra stress.

She was still dealing with the ripples Jesse had made

in her pond. Tad was fretful and argumentative a good deal of the time lately, furious that he couldn't see Jesse. He was more aggressively interested in football than ever too. At least she hoped he got all his various cuts and bruises from playing football and not from fighting. She'd find out next week. His teacher had asked her to come in for a conference.

Olivia was treating her with an angry solicitude that made her want to scream. In fact, she often felt like screaming lately. She wasn't herself at all.

Or was she? she wondered. Maybe the serene, controlled person she'd been showing the world the last few years wasn't really her. She was restless. A lot of soothing routine tasks just seemed tedious to her these days. She was tired of turning out the same meringue shells over and over, making the same salad dressing day after day.

She was lonely too. Where before she'd accepted invitations reluctantly, she now found herself seeking people out. She could handle social occasions; it was being alone she was having trouble with. In fact, it was she who'd called Garrett. After refusing his invitations for weeks, she'd made his day when she'd phoned.

Obviously, the evening wasn't coming up to his expectations, though. He reached across the table for her hand. "Bettina, you'll blow me away with all these sighs. What's wrong?" He laughed, but he sounded more irritated than amused.

She flashed him a quick smile. "Sorry. Tad told me today he was 'having a mood.' Maybe I'm having one too. Have you decided what you're going to eat?"

They ordered, and Garrett poured a glass of wine for her. He kissed her hand, then said, "Try this. I think you'll like it." He was making a lot of excuses to take her hand tonight.

With the glass halfway to her lips, Betsy froze, her gaze fixed on the entrance to the restaurant. A man who was six foot three with enormous shoulders and golden hair followed a beautiful platinum blonde into the dining room.

Betsy knew immediately that the woman was Jesse's mother. They had the same cheekbones and the same quality of self-control in the way they held themselves. For a moment she felt dizzy. Her ears began to ring and hot blood rushed to her head, obliterating her senses, so that she stared straight at Jesse but saw nothing for several seconds. Then the heat wave ebbed, leaving her shaken. It happened quicker than thought and told her more surely than a week's thinking could have that she loved Jesse Kincaid, body and soul, and always would.

Oh, damn! She'd been careful, logical, and rational when she'd fallen in love this time, and she'd thrown away the only thing that made life worth living. Despair swept through her. Jesse's life wasn't for her, but how could she live without him?

She couldn't take her eyes off him. He looked as smooth and clean as Garrett. No, she corrected herself, he was all angles and hard, slicing edges, even in a tailored suit. You couldn't call Jesse smooth.

All emotion had been ironed out of his expression. She'd never seen him look that way before. She shivered, hating it.

Jesse saw Betsy. His eyes narrowed intently, scanning her face, her slim black dress, her hair pinned up in a chignon, and her hand in Garrett's. She looked sophisticated and sexy as hell. For a minute, before the aloof mask fell back into place, he wasn't emotionless at all. *No!* something shouted in his mind. He'd thought he could leave her alone, but not if she was going to let yuppies in three-piece suits paw her. She could stay in her ivory tower if she wanted, but no one else was going to touch her!

Betsy saw him stop his mother and say something to her, gesturing toward her and Garrett. His mother in turn halted the maître d'. The man nodded as they veered off.

Garrett had turned to see what Betsy was staring at. "Isn't that Jesse Kincaid?" he asked, noticeably impressed.

"Yes," Betsy answered in a low voice.

It was clear the Kincaids were coming toward them. Garrett looked swiftly from them to Betsy and back again. "Then it *was* you in that photograph with Jesse Kincaid!" He was dumbfounded. Obviously he'd seen the picture but had refused to believe it was Betsy.

"It wasn't what it looked like, Garrett," she murmured.

Liar! It was more, she admitted miserably to herself. Much more.

Garrett had hidden his astonishment by the time Jesse halted at their table.

Flushed and shaky, Betsy looked up, and up, at brown eyes that watched her inscrutably. Jesse's control was firmly in place. Garrett scraped his chair back and stood in deference to Mrs. Kincaid.

"Betsy," Jesse said, nodding. "I'd like you to meet my mother. Mother, this is Bettina Carmody."

Betsy held out her hand to the elegant woman who had Jesse's cheekbones. "Hello, Mrs. Kincaid."

Icy blue eyes measured her before a gloved hand reached out to accept hers. "How do you do?"

"Mrs. Kincaid, this is Garrett Phillips. Garrett, Jesse Kincaid."

Jesse nodded affably at Garrett but made no move to shake hands, or to leave. The silence stretched on.

"Won't you sit down?" Garrett said politely. "We just ordered. Unless you . . ."

"Thank you," Jesse said, smiling silkily. "We'd be delighted, wouldn't we, Mother?"

Jessica Kincaid inclined her head graciously. "Indeed."

Betsy glanced from one Kincaid to the other, ending with a puzzled frown at Jesse. What was he playing at? She'd choke if she had to eat dinner with him tonight after all that had happened between them.

He signaled the waiter for extra chairs. "Now we can find out from an expert what's good here," he said coolly. She slid him an indignant look. He knew she didn't want him there.

"Nightshade's said to be fine this season," she murmured in a voice only he was likely to hear. His lips turned up slightly.

"What's that, Ms. Carmody?" Jessica Kincaid asked, allowing Jesse to seat her.

Louder, Betsy said, "Bernie does some nice things with mushrooms for appetizers."

Jesse and his mother ordered. Then he looked assessingly at Garrett.

"Tad tells me you're a stockbroker, Mr. Phillips. You and my mother have a lot in common."

Jessica Kincaid had been watching her son impassively. Now she leaned forward and asked, "What do you think, Mr. Phillips, of a man who puts all his money in mutual funds with a stockbroker as a mother?"

Betsy watched mother and son, chilled by the cynical familiarity in their manner toward each other.

At his obsequious worst, Garrett babbled, "When the broker is Jessica Kincaid, I'd have to say he's out of his mind." He knew of Jessica Kincaid, of course. Everyone doing business in the city did. To an up-and-coming stockbroker a contact with Kincaid Enterprises could be a big boost.

Jesse eyed him thoughtfully. "You'd have made a good Kincaid, Mr. Phillips." Garrett smiled. Only Betsy realized the disdain behind that remark.

The first course arrived, providing a distraction. After a couple of bites of melon and prosciutto, Betsy abandoned the idea of eating. The lime juice flavoring the food felt like battery acid in her throat.

"I have to thank you for your recommendation, Ms. Carmody," Jessica Kincaid said, delicately carving a mushroom cap into slivers. "These stuffed mushrooms are delicious."

Garrett was enjoying his snails, but Jesse pushed pâté around on his plate abstractedly.

Betsy studied him, wondering what had caused him to look so exhausted. It was incredibly painful, his being just across the table and yet so far away. She missed having him smile at her, knowing they were on the same wavelength. She missed everything about the way it had been between them.

He leaned back in his chair, sipping his usual seltzer. "How have you been, Betsy?" he asked under cover of a conversation between Garrett and his mother.

"Fine, Jesse. How about you?"

"Good, good," he said, thinking she probably didn't even realize she was twisting her napkin compulsively in her lap. "How's Tad?"

"The same."

They watched each other warily. Betsy thought she couldn't stand much more. She'd rather have him screaming at her than asking polite, meaningless questions.

"Life been peaceful at Calcuisine lately? Read any good cookbooks?"

Her eyes flashed. She'd wanted him to talk about something real, but if he was going to sneer at her profession . . . "How about you? Having fun playing with balls? I see you've been making headlines as usual."

One corner of his mouth lifted in a lopsided grin. He'd made sports headlines, but he could tell by the hint of jealousy in her voice that she was talking about the other headline, the one describing how he'd crowned the Winter Festival queen and had gotten a very physical thank-you. "I'm surprised you were interested enough to read the captions," he said.

"There's an awful fascination with the celebrity life." She wondered as she spoke why she was letting him get a rise out of her. She didn't want the rift between them to grow any wider.

He must have felt the same, because he shrugged and said, "Headlines are an occupational hazard. It doesn't mean anything. Reporters come with the shoulder pads and cleats."

"Don't look now, but there's one heading this way."

Jesse quickly masked the look of disgust in his eyes, as Janet Larson approached their table.

"Hello, Jesse!" Delight and surprise made Janet Larson's beautiful face even more appealing. "Mrs. Kincaid." She nodded to the older woman.

"Good evening, Janet."

Janet presented her date and eyed Betsy with bright,

interested eyes. "Aren't you going to introduce me to your friends, Jesse?"

He looked at her with tolerant amusement. "Are you off duty, Janet?"

She seemed momentarily displeased, then gave a tinkling laugh. "I'm never off duty, Jesse. You know that."

"I do indeed." He and the lovely reporter stared at each other with challenging smiles. Finally, she laughed rather angrily. "All right, be secretive. I'll find out anyway, you know."

Jesse just smiled. "Enjoy your meal."

When Janet and her date had gone, he said to Betsy, "You were almost a headline yourself."

"Thank you for keeping me out of print."

"You're welcome. I am fairly good at protecting myself from the press, you know. They print a lot of things about me, but rarely anything I don't want them to."

"Now there's a waste of talent," Jessica Kincaid said tartly. "He could have been a diplomat, but instead he plays games with reporters."

The gibe didn't bother Jesse. He watched Betsy for her reaction to the incident, though.

She nodded thoughtfully. Maybe she'd overreacted to the public side of Jesse's life, she mused. Seeing him with Janet Larson, she hadn't experienced any of the jealousy she'd felt watching them together on television. It was possible she'd blown other parts of his life out of proportion, too, in reaction to her own experiences. The last year of Brian's life, when his extracurricular social life had been big news, she'd felt she couldn't go out of the house without people whispering about Brian Carmody's poor, abandoned wife.

Their waiter delivered the entrees and made a production of arranging them. Betsy hardly noticed. Her mind was working furiously.

Here Jesse was, she thought, at the best restaurant in San Francisco, and except when he was sparring with her he looked bored stiff. Was she wrong about him? Maybe what they wanted out of life wasn't so very different.

"How's the salmon, Bettina?" Garrett asked.

"What? Oh, it's . . . I guess it's fine." She looked at her untouched meal and forced herself to take a bite.

Garrett leaned toward Mrs. Kincaid, who was proving to be his best audience tonight. "I remember the first time I ever tasted Coho salmon. It was in Seattle . . ."

For once Betsy was glad of Garrett's interminable stories. He could carry the conversation while she just sat there and thought. She had a lot to think about. She stared at Jesse, who was eating without interest.

She remembered his going off light-heartedly for a sail with Tad, picnicking in the vineyards, roughhousing on Marina green. As if something compelled her, she leaned toward him and said in a low voice, "You were happy washing dishes in my kitchen, weren't you?"

It should have seemed like a strange question, but he instantly understood her meaning. "Utterly," he said, looking at her watchfully. She nodded, satisfied, and leaned back in her chair. Still watching her, Jesse resumed cutting his filet mignon. Betsy stared at the wall, feeling she was on the brink of an important insight into Jesse's character.

With his mother and Garrett, with Janet Larson, with most of his teammates, Jesse talked and smiled, but it was all surface charm. She marveled that people didn't know they weren't really seeing him at all. He had a self-protective facade that made hers look flimsy. The difference between the way he was with most of the world and the way he was with Hap, or with Tad, but most of all with her, was the difference between being clothed and unclothed.

Suddenly she had a flash of realization that made her sit up straight in her seat. Jesse's violent rage the last time they'd met had to be a measure of his feelings for him. He cared too much to be calm and reasonable. It was a sign of love. She couldn't imagine him shouting at his mother, for instance.

She stared wide-eyed at Jesse. He looked up from his plate and stopped cutting, his knife and fork buried in the rare meat. There was no change in his position, but his chest visibly rose and fell. Would they always have this ability to engage each other's feelings with just a look? Betsy wondered. She continued to stare as she struggled to file away this shocking, earth-shaking realization until she could think about it later. Jesse loved her. Maybe they could have more than an affair. Maybe it could work. Her mind whirled.

"What?" he asked softly.

"Jesse, have I made a terrible mistake?" she whispered.

His gaze fastened on hers. He didn't answer right away, but when he did it was with a trace of bitterness. "I couldn't give you an unbiased answer, I'm afraid."

She sat back, stunned. Did he know what she was asking? She thought he did, and she knew he loved her. But he refused to help her out of the impasse she'd created. He'd come after her before in spite of her objections, but not this time. He would only take so much rejection.

Betsy couldn't have said what happened during the rest of the meal. She supposed she'd answered remarks without embarrassing herself. No one had stared or commented, at any rate. But what was going on around her had so little meaning compared to what was happening in her head that she simply couldn't be bothered with it.

The first thing that really penetrated, besides Jesse watching her, was Jessica Kincaid announcing, "I would like to go, now, Jesse."

"You don't want dessert or coffee, Mother?" Jesse asked mildly.

"No, thank you."

Jesse rose to his feet and held out his hand to Garrett. "Well, then, we'll say good night. Thank you for sharing your table. A pleasure to meet you."

"My pleasure," Garrett insisted. "And you, Mrs. Kincaid. I hope we'll meet again."

Jessica Kincaid inclined her head graciously. "Possibly we shall." To Betsy she said simply, "Good-bye."

"Good-bye," Betsy murmured. She looked at Jesse. His dark eyes told her nothing. She didn't know what her own eyes were communicating. She didn't really care. If they were alone she'd tell him. That she loved him. That she'd try to be braver. That she hadn't had a happy second in the last two weeks and that since he didn't look very happy himself, didn't he think they should give it another try?

It was a long look. Jessica Kincaid waited serenely, but Garrett fidgeted, shifting from one foot to another.

"Good-bye, Betsy," Jesse said slowly.

"Good-bye." It came out weak and tentative.

She watched him escort his mother out the door.

She wished he hadn't said good-bye. It sounded so final. She wished he'd said, see you. Even if it was a threat.

She should have said, see you, she thought. She'd thrown his love for her in his face. It was up to her, now.

She turned to her date. "Could we leave, too, Garrett? There are some things I need to do."

Fourteen

Brrr! Betsy shivered and hunched her knees up to her chin, trying to huddle deeper into the alcove at Jesse's front door. The coat she'd worn to Bernie's was velvet and elegant, but for this weather she needed a parka. When she'd picked up her car and asked Tad's babysitter to stay overnight, she hadn't considered that she might be waiting for Jesse on the street.

She checked her watch in the light from the streetlamp. Midnight. He would be home soon, unless he was spending the night somewhere else.

No. It was that kind of thinking that had made her send Jesse away in the first place. She wouldn't give in to it now.

She turned to check the house number. Maybe she had the wrong place? No, this was it.

She heard a car approaching and willed herself not to lean forward and look. There'd been at least fifty cars since she'd been here, and they'd all rumbled on by. She sagged at the swish that told her this one had passed too.

Because she'd been expecting a car, she didn't react to the footsteps except to huddle closer against the door. She didn't need trouble from midnight prowlers.

But the footsteps turned into the cul-de-sac and grew

louder. They were slower than usual, but as they came closer she recognized them as Jesse's. That gave her a few seconds' warning, but even so her heart was pounding uncomfortably when Jesse's dark bulk came into sight. He was looking down at the pavement, but at the foot of the stairs he looked up and halted.

Betsy cleared her throat. "Where have you been?" she asked nervously. "I'm frozen."

She was thinking, please don't say anything horrid. She knew what her being here might look like. The seconds ticked by as Jesse stared at Betsy. He was struggling with the impulse to crush her to him, to swing her around and to say, "Welcome home, and don't ever do that to me again." But he had to be sure why she was here. If she thought she could kiss and run again, she'd find out just how wrong she was. He climbed the stairs, reaching in his pocket for his keys. "I've been walking," he said. "Come inside, we'll both get warm."

She stood and brushed dirt from the back of her coat. "You mean I've been waiting all this time for a car that was here all along?"

He looked sideways at her as he swung the door open. He gestured her inside, then followed. "Was it the car you were waiting for?"

She expelled a tense breath. It was all up to her. He wasn't going to make it easy.

"No," she said, turning to face him. "It was the man."

He smiled at that. A slow, not terribly happy smile. She resisted the urge to put a hand on his cheek.

"May I take off my coat?" she asked.

He nodded, reaching in a closet for a hanger. He hung both their coats with deliberation while Betsy stood there, wanting to shift from foot to foot or yell at him. "Come on, I'll make some coffee," he said.

She followed him through a living room that looked out over the Bay. Making a swift survey, she saw that the room was large, modern, and austere, with just a few pieces of good furniture, and good art on the walls. Not her style, but if she'd gone for ultramodern, it might have been. She stopped at a wall of bookshelves and scanned the titles. Plato. *Future Shock. The Book of Laughter and Forgetting*, by Milan Kundera. She pulled out that last one, observing that it was well thumbed. The man actually read.

Beyond the glass doors a deck overhung the quarried cliffs above the Embarcadero. Jesse had several miles of some of the most expensive real estate in the world at his feet.

From the kitchen he called, "Do you want decaf or regular?"

"Doesn't matter," she replied, following his voice. "Whatever you're having." She doubted she'd sleep much that night anyhow.

She slid onto a stool while Jesse moved around his small, highly technical kitchen. Looking at the electric can opener, knife sharpener, and so on, she asked, "Do you provide a testing service for manufacturers of electrical appliances?"

"I'm a lazy man. You purists can do it the hard way."

He put cups, sugar, and cream on a tray and led the way into the living room. "The view's nice from here at night." He set her cup on the coffee table in front of the couch. He took his own to a sleek leather-and-chrome reclining chair. His legs stretched toward her, making his face seem far away.

They sipped, watching each other over the rims of their cups. Betsy was struck again by Jesse's haggardness. Impulsively she asked, "Jesse, what's wrong? You look terrible." To make him smile, she added, "Your mother's not that bad."

He didn't smile, but he didn't put her off. His eyes darkened with pain as he set his cup down. "Partly it's that I'm missing you and Tad," he said slowly. "But that's more of a constant ache." He paused. "Partly . . ." He took and released a deep breath. "Partly it's because I lost a child in the emergency room today."

A cry burst from Betsy and she was across the room and on her knees beside his chair. Her arms closed around him, her head pressed against his chest. His eyes closed, and beneath her she felt his body heave once, and then a second time. She held him while he cried silently. She put all the strength she had into holding him and loving him.

She'd always seen him as a warrior. Now in her mind there was a vision of him as a different kind of warrior. She knew he'd be as uncompromising fighting for a child's life as he was on the football field. She'd seen him with children, and she knew how he felt about them. "Oh, Jesse," she murmured. "Oh, Jesse."

At length he was still again. She continued to hold him closely. "Was it the first patient you've lost?" she asked finally, thinking it might ease him to talk about it.

"No, working in the emergency room you do lose someone once in a while. But it was the first child. A little girl, about four." There was agony in his quiet voice.

Her arms tightened in shared grief. He lifted his to encircle her. They held each other a long time, breathing quietly. Eventually, sensing a change in him, she lifted her head to look into his dark eyes.

"I need you, Betsy," he said. "I want to love you." Whatever thoughts he'd had about challenging her motives for being here were gone. He felt the universal urge to seek life as an antidote to death. He wanted to bury himself in her.

Jesse wasn't a taker. He'd never before used a woman for comfort or forgetfulness. If his mother had taught him one thing, it was not to let anyone make a weapon of your feelings. This, though, was so natural and right, he didn't even think about it. He knew he could trust Betsy.

She smiled her love at him. "Yes," she said. She stood and offered her hand. He led her down a hall whose carpet muffled their footsteps. They entered a bedroom and continued through it to a small deck with a sunken tub on it. It was made private by a wall of one-way glass.

He stooped to remove the cover from the tub. Tendrils of steam coiled upward and disappeared into the cool night air.

"In there?" Betsy said dubiously.

"All right?" he asked, looking up at her.

She smiled. "A bit upscale for me, but why not? It's California, after all."

"It's hydrotherapy, for me," he said, rising and bringing her lightly against his chest. His bottomless, grief-circled eyes fastened on hers as if he could draw what he needed from them. "Every time I've been in there the last two months, I've imagined you. I want the real thing."

He reached for the pins that held her hair in the chignon. It tumbled over his hands with a flash of red. He clutched thick fistfuls of the silky mass, lifting it to his face and breathing deeply. "You smell like wildflowers and cool breezes." His voice was deep and rough.

She loosened his tie, saying in a siren voice, "You smell like a man."

His hand swept down her back, taking her zipper with it. With nimble fingers she slid buttons through holes. In minutes they stood shivering in the night air.

Jesse's bruise looked better—yellow mottled with pink instead of deep purple and green. She lifted a hand and smoothed it gently over what seemed like acres of chest and shoulder. "Does that hurt?" she asked.

He covered her hand with his and pressed. "No. You don't have to be careful."

A smile spread over her face as her mind echoed and reinterpreted his statement. For the first time since she'd met Jesse, she'd lowered her guard. She'd come here determined to open up to him in spite of her fears, but that all seemed a little silly now. Jesse's courage humbled her. Vulnerability and openness were gifts you gave to the people you loved.

"I think I'm through being careful," she whispered, turning her hand beneath his so that their fingers meshed and gripped. He searched her eyes for confirmation of the words. She stood on tiptoe and lifted her face for his kiss. Gently he lowered his lips to hers and tasted. He raised his face an inch to study her, then dipped again and clung.

Her mouth opened under his as her tongue delicately edged his bottom lip. Against their joined hands he could feel her breasts. His fingers clenched convulsively and his other hand swept down her body from shoulder to buttocks, drawing a smothered sigh. He felt goosebumps on her skin and pulled away. "You're cold. Come into the water."

Still holding her hand, he led the way into the hot tub. She watched his torso slide out of sight with regret. "You should put lights in this thing," she murmured.

He grinned, admiring her over his shoulder. "Maybe I will. Why don't you just stand out there awhile so I can see you?"

She shivered in the clear, cold night air. "No, thank you. Make room."

The water was warm. It lapped about her legs by degrees as she descended the tread-lined fiberglass steps to the bottom of the tub. Jesse sank onto the seat edge with an "ah-h-h" of relaxation and pulled her down next to him. Water covered all but their heads and necks, sending up a faint smell of chlorine. Jesse slid down farther so that the back of his head rested on the tub's rim, then turned to look at Betsy.

She gazed back, feeling she could stare at him forever. There was such strength in his jaw and clean-cut nose, so much intelligence in his steady brown eyes. She traced the slashes in his cheeks with a wet finger, leaving snail-tracks of moisture. The marks disappeared as a smile deepened the creases into crevices. Her fingers made a path to his eyes, wanting to touch the thick, short lashes. As she trailed water along his eyelids, they closed and the lashes separated into spiky clumps.

Heat penetrated and loosened Betsy's muscles. She drew steamy air into her lungs and felt languor steal over her. She wanted to touch every part of Jesse, to gentle him and let her fingers tell of her love.

He sighed and slid down another inch. She caressed his eyebrows, cheekbones, and lips with her fingertips, reading sorrow and vulnerability beneath the sensuality in his face. "Jesse, Jesse," she crooned softly.

She'd been on the defensive since she'd met him, she realized, and that had made her slow to recognize his needs. Funny. If she'd just discovered earlier how hungry he was for the love she and Tad took for granted, she wouldn't have resisted him so hard.

"Betsy," he murmured. It was like a prayer of gratitude.

She smiled. "Yes, love," she said joyfully. She placed her lips on his, just holding them there before she began kissing him lightly.

She hadn't understood before what she had that he could want, but she knew now. He'd probably never shown this side of himself to anyone else. She doubted if he'd ever asked anyone for anything before.

He was communicating now. He moaned and his tongue flicked her lips as she kissed him. She obediently deepened the kiss. His stomach muscles clenched as her hand slid over him, and she followed the subtle signals the slight shifts of his body sent her. She knew where he wanted her to touch him, and how.

His need of her created such a strength of love she felt invincible. A humming grew in her body. She put her hands behind him and lifted. "Float for a minute," she murmured.

"I float like lead," he said, but still stretched out atop the water. She laughed in delight at all his quiescent power sprawling there like a finely-tuned machine waiting to be started. His golden chest hairs drifted on the water as wavelets slapped gently at his horizontal body. Her hands slipped over him to caress and explore. As her lips followed, touching and tasting, gutteral sounds rumbled deep in his chest and throat. His eyes were open, but blind, and his breathing grew stertorous.

Eventually, he turned his face to her. As if commanded, she lifted her head. Jesse's eyes flashed at the sight of her sensual, softly parted lips and the water-dipped tips of her hair. With a subdued roar, he reached for her, and the passivity was gone. He pulled, and she slid over him. He followed after her, his mouth chasing her down so that for a moment he drove her underwater. They came up laughing and gasping.

Water sloshed over the side of the tub as they lunged and rolled. Betsy gulped for breath. All Jesse's vulnerability had changed to drive. There was something primitive about the sheer animal power of him, but tenderness made a glory of the galloping course they were on.

He kissed and possessed her mouth again and again, demanding, insisting, while his hands made her body a helpless, throbbing thing. His fingers tangled in her hair, above and below, and the tug was echoed by a tug of desire so sharp it arched her out of the water. He held her so he could feast on the perfect curve and swell of her breasts. The biting air was a shock after the hot moisture, pulling her nipples into a taut invitation before his lips and tongue provided another kind of heat.

As reaction surged through Betsy, she bucked, churning the water violently. Water droplets spangled her lashes, so that she saw Jesse's fierce brown gaze through a rainbow haze. She cried out in unbearable excitement. For the first time in her life, she was totally open to her sexuality, and if she'd been capable of thought she'd have been astonished at the depths of her response.

Jesse stood up, the water to his waist, and wrapped her legs around him. She reached behind her for the support of the rim and held on.

His intent gaze roamed the slender, creamy-skinned body spread out in front of him and the drifting mermaid hair before it fastened insistently on her wide, eager green eyes. Those eyes mirrored the difference he'd sensed in her. Here was that glorious, giving womanliness he'd always recognized, allied with a confidence that increased its power tenfold.

He could demand, for the first time, instead of cajoling or wooing her. He'd hoped she was through running, when he'd found her on the steps. He'd half believed she was when she'd made love to him so sweetly and sensually. But he knew now, for certain. There was nothing tentative or reluctant about this loving. Betsy was participating with every nerve, offering him commitment with every sigh and movement. He didn't have to worry she'd misinterpret his forcefulness. There was as much power in her as in him. She could have him groveling if she liked.

"Ah, Betsy," he said raggedly, "you steal the heart out of me."

She smiled in slumbrous allure. He growled deep in his throat as he joined their bodies with a powerful thrust. She cried out, but her eyes remained open, brimful of wonder. He began to move, and water thumped and slapped at the sides of the tub.

"Jesse," she whispered as her eyes closed. Other senses took precedence. She was surfing through waves of sensation, clinging with her thighs to Jesse like a sea goddess riding on the crest of a forty-foot wave in a night-time ocean. For a split second she was sure she'd be destroyed when the wave crashed, then it didn't matter. She went with the ecstasy of the ride, one step ahead of the curl of limitless power, till it caught them. Stars exploded above her head as the wall of water crashed, rolling and tumbling them in a surge of mind-crushing force.

Afterward, they floated on the surface of the water, rocked gently by any small movement, and watched the lights of the city and of Berkeley across the bay. A couple of ships slipped silently out toward the Golden Gate. The mournful bleat of a foghorn drifted up to them, and a dog barked nearby.

A late fog was rolling in from the ocean, obliterating the stars as they watched. The moon slid behind the cloud blanket, then briefly reappeared to cast a silver swath across the water of the hot tub. Betsy sighed in complete contentment. The sound drew a smile from Jesse.

"Well, how about it?" he teased. "Aren't you going to tell me that was nice?"

Her lips hardly moved as she said fondly, "Shut up."

When the fog shrouded their view and muffled the sounds of the city, Jesse stirred. "After a while, you're not sure if this is relaxing or just enervating."

"I know what you mean."

He reared half out of the water and lifted himself to the deck in one fluid motion.

"Hey!" she said as his wake rocked her violently.

He grinned. "Do you think you could walk to the bedroom?"

"Not in a straight line." She held up a hand and allowed him to haul her out.

He took a huge towel from a nearby stack and tenderly wrapped her in it, sarong style. He tucked another towel around his own waist. Draping an arm over her shoulder, he said, "Come on."

They lay in the darkness, Jesse on his back, Betsy on her stomach with an arm across his chest. There was such closeness between them, she felt that talking about their relationship had become superfluous. It seemed years ago that they were staring at each other across miles of pink linen tablecloth. She smiled, remembering, and raised her head to look at him. "You ruined poor Garrett's evening, you know."

Jesse opened one eye and made a "hmmmpf" in his throat. " 'Poor Garrett' was holding your hand."

She raised her brows, saying, so?

He closed the eye and said expressionlessly, "I wanted to take his head off." His mouth twitched as he added, "But since you showed up here, I've decided to let him live."

"Magnanimous," she murmured.

He turned his head to look at her. "I'm a mild-mannered guy in general, you know."

She smiled, realizing that he probably believed that. Few enough people had tapped into that volcanic core that he probably didn't even realize it was central to him.

"Uh-huh," she agreed in a tone of disbelief.

He smiled wryly. After a pause, he said, "I was fairly uncivilized to you the night I brought Tad back from the game, wasn't I?"

Another, more emphatic "Uh-huh."

He looked away, thinking. "It's only with you that I lose control. With everyone else, I have the reputation of being a cool character."

Another "Uh-huh," this one amused.

He glanced at her. "You don't believe me?"

"Oh, I believe you! But I don't know why you should think it's reassuring that you're a maniac only with me."

He grinned and nuzzled her neck. "Maybe it's a warning. You'll have to be careful not to rile me, won't you?"

She laughed. "I'll walk on tiptoe."

It was his turn for a skeptical, "Uh-huh."

She shifted, settling more comfortably against him. Just the feel of him brought such delight.

He was still thinking about the meeting in the restaurant. "Mother approved of you," he said ironically.

"It's not mutual, though I pity her. It must have been awful, growing up with your mother."

He chuckled. "I always imagined it was a little like finishing school. 'Stand up straight, Jesse. Be a gentleman. Don't gobble.' "

"Oh, you had the same appetite then?" Betsy said treacherously. He put a hand on her throat in pretended menace.

More seriously, she asked, "Is that what attracted you to football? It was so different from your mother's world?"

He looked surprised. "Maybe it was. It always seemed refreshingly real."

"Your mother must hate it." As she spoke, Betsy experienced a small pang. She hated it, too. She and Jessica Kincaid had that in common.

"She loathes it," Jesse said with satisfaction. "Gracie, now, she's a fan." His voice held a deep warmth.

"Do you still see her?" Betsy asked, curious about this woman he seemed to love so much.

"Every year, during the off season. When we were in the Super Bowl, I flew her in. She still answers my letters the day she gets them, and still scolds me."

A warm feeling for Gracie rose in Betsy. "I'd like to meet her."

"You will," he promised her.

She picked up his hand to look at his Super Bowl ring. "You've accomplished it all in football, haven't you?"

He studied her. She wanted to believe that, he knew. "I'm a greedy bastard," he said softly. "I want another one."

She nodded, getting the message and feeling a flutter of uneasiness. Then she smiled. She wouldn't let anything build into an issue between them. Whatever their differences, she felt they could handle them now.

He relaxed when he saw her smile. Then she tucked her head into the crook of his shoulder and he closed his eyes. "Tad's missing you," she said.

It was a minute before Jesse said, "I miss him, too."

"I think he's been fighting at school. His teacher asked me to come in for a conference next week."

He was silent. "I should make you come, too," she said. "It's really your fault."

He raised his head to look at her. If she meant what he thought she did, it was a major concession. "You'd let me go?"

She bit her lip and nodded. "But you probably can't get out of practice, can you?"

He shook his head. They both knew that wasn't the point. "I'll go to the next one," he promised. She smiled and relaxed against him.

"Do you suppose Tad'll be jealous of the new baby?" he asked.

She gave a shocked little laugh. "Do you know something I don't?"

He was grinning, but there was a slight anxiousness behind his words. "You do want more children, don't you?"

She nodded, thinking how strange it was that the idea of having Jesse's babies wasn't new to her. "Three?" she suggested.

"I've always thought four. Five, with Tad."

She considered that, then said with her head to one side, "Okay. I guess we can afford to send them to college."

"Good," he said with satisfaction. "I want children, but I'd have married you even if you'd said no."

She rose up in high indignation. "Too kind!" she exclaimed sarcastically. He chuckled.

They lay together in their fog-insulated world, happiness possessing them. Betsy's fingers stroked Jesse's face, feeling the stubble appearing there and enjoying the angles and creases. Jesse smoothed his hand slowly up and down her back, loosening her towel.

"Do you realize," he said, "that we hardly ever make love in a proper bed? I don't count that Victorian mushbasket of Fred's."

"Hmmm, I liked that bed. This is a bit Spartan for my tastes. Hard and unyielding, like you." She wrinkled her nose at him.

He laughed. "I suppose we'll have to live in your house, but I'm bringing my bed."

"I knew you'd take over my life," she said contentedly. "The house will never be the same."

He rolled over, pulling her so that they reversed positions. Looking down into her face with warm eyes, he touched her nose with the tip of a finger. "We'll compromise, but you'll always be your own woman, Betsy. I promise you that."

She nodded, a smile slowly growing. "I'll be my own woman," she agreed. "And yours."

Fifteen

The next morning Jesse insisted on making breakfast. "I know darn well you've done more cooking than I have this week."

Betsy smiled and let him have his way. "This could be the real crisis in our relationship, you know."

"Piece of cake," he bragged. "My Acapulco omelette would melt harder hearts than yours. Set the table on the deck, why don't you?"

Half an hour later Betsy swallowed her last bite of egg with artichoke and peppers and leaned back in her chair. "You pass. That was delicious."

Jesse smiled smugly and refilled her coffee cup. She sipped in quiet contentment, enjoying the cool freshness of the morning air, the raucous cries of the gulls wheeling off the cliffs, and Jesse's company.

They watched the fog thin and blue patches appear. Jesse scanned the sky assessingly, and she knew his attention had shifted to the game ahead. It was the first game of the play-offs and maybe the toughest.

Half to himself he said, "It's clearing. That's good. We have enough to worry about without rain or mud."

"The Gators have a reputation for dirty play, don't they?" she asked nervously.

He looked at her. "Physical," he amended with a hint of irony.

"Do you think you'll win?"

He grinned. "I always think we'll win."

She smiled back. "Maybe that's why you usually do."

Jesse wouldn't even let her clear the kitchen. "I like to keep busy before a game," he said.

He was more jittery than she'd ever seen him, roaming the apartment picking things up, compulsively making order.

She sat on the couch, idling thumbing through the morning paper and watching him from the corners of her eyes. She felt her own anxiety growing with his restlessness and bit her lip, wondering if she should leave. These were the day-to-day things you had to learn about someone to make a marriage work. Could she give him what he needed at times like these? Could she keep her own fears under control?

She felt sick when she thought about watching today's game on television. Uh-uh. Not this one, she decided. She didn't think their relationship could stand it.

When Jesse had paced the living room five more times and rejected her offer of a walk, she decided she'd had enough. She folded the paper and rose to her feet. "Jesse, I'm going. I want to see Tad before he leaves for Candelero."

Jesse stopped pacing and looked at her, a frown drawing creases between his eyebrows. "Aren't you coming to the game?"

She tried to read his voice. It was a fairly curt question. Was there wistfulness in it? Would it help him, she wondered, knowing she was there? Could she stand it? "Do you want me to come?" she asked, her tone slightly shrill in spite of all she could do to control it.

The frown deepened. He hesitated about half a second before he shook his head. "No." Another half second and he repeated it in a stronger voice. "No, I wouldn't want you to go through that. Not yet."

Relieved, she said apologetically, "I probably wouldn't be much use."

He came to her and put his hands on her shoulders, then kissed her on the forehead. "I'm not much good the day of a game myself. It's probably best just to stay out of my way. I love you, you know." He was apologizing for shutting her out.

"I know," she said softly, standing on tiptoe to kiss his lips. "Will you come by after the game?" If he was in one piece, she added silently.

He nodded. "Tell Alex and Tad I'll give them a ride if they wait."

"Okay." Indecisive, she bit her lip. "Well, 'bye." When she made no move to go, he smiled indulgently and gave her a little shove. "Come on, I'll walk you to your car. You don't have to hold my hand all the time."

Tad was ecstatic when Betsy told him Jesse would bring him home. "Yippee!" He produced the first wholehearted smile she'd seen on him in weeks.

"Yippee," repeated Olivia, who'd brought Alex over to pick up Tad.

"You're sure you don't want the third ticket?" Betsy asked her.

Olivia shook her head. "You remember Leon?"

Betsy remembered. He was a glib and charming microfilm salesman who breezed into and out of Olivia's life twice a year.

"He's taking me to the park for the day," Olivia said.

"What about Warren?" Betsy asked.

Olivia sniffed. "Warren needs shaking up. Football players are arrogant." Realizing what she'd said, she hastened to add, "Except Jesse, of course."

Betsy laughed. "Jesse's the most arrogant of the bunch."

"He is not!" Tad defended his hero staunchly.

Betsy smiled and ruffled her son's hair. "He'd be the first to admit it. Ask him yourself tonight."

• • •

For once Betsy didn't have a catering job on a Sunday. She washed her hair, did her nails, and took time grooming herself and dressing in her favorite camel-colored slacks and sweater. She stuffed a goat-cheese-and-leek filling under the skin of a roasting chicken for the evening meal and thawed one of the mocha tortes Jesse had liked so much.

When she ran out of things to do, she stood at the French doors of the kitchen, looking out at bright sunshine in the garden and feeling as if it should be raining. Why was she so uneasy? she asked herself. It was just another football game. Jesse had played in hundreds. He'd play in another fifty, if he had his way. What was the problem?

Nothing. No problem, she assured herself. Just an incurable congenital hatred of football.

Staring at a bed of late zinnias, she saw instead Jesse despairing over a dead child. Her uneasiness grew. She remembered him saying he wished her anxiety at the Ranger game had been for him.

You selfish idiot! she told herself through a rising fear. Of course he wouldn't tell her he wanted her at the game. She'd made it abundantly clear she hated football, and he cared how she felt.

What about her? Did she care how he felt? He needed her support. She was the one he trusted with his feelings. He was risking his body, so surely it would help if someone else there cared as much as he did.

She thought about her resolution to be braver. How far was she willing to go with that? Just far enough to let Jesse share her life, but not far enough to share his? Was that her idea of love? Her mouth firmed as she wheeled and marched down the hall. Before she could talk herself out of it, she snatched up purse and coat and slammed the front door behind her. She had the extra ticket; she could make it by halftime. She'd shout. He'd know she was there for the second half at least.

She drove fast, feeling a sense of urgency. Her hands on the wheel were icy. She'd have given anything to have gone with Tad and Alex. She had a dreadful feeling now that something awful would happen and she wouldn't be there when Jesse needed her. How could she have considered staying away when he was in danger?

She parked in an illegal zone, not caring in the least if she got a ticket. They could tow the car away if they liked. She wasn't hiking a half hour to get to the stadium.

Tad and Alex looked up in surprise as she slipped into the vacant seat beside them.

"Betsy!"

"Mom! What are you doing here?"

"I came to watch the game," she said with a false breeziness. "Who's winning?"

"We are." Tad was scornful that she should even ask such a thing. If Jesse was playing, of course they were winning.

Alex filled her in. "Ten point lead. Jesse's been fantastic. It's second down and a little under two minutes to play in the half. The Gators'll expect 'em to run it, to keep them from getting the ball, but I don't know. Jesse's so hot, if I were the coach, I'd go for another touchdown."

"I hope they run it," Betsy murmured. She glanced at the game clock, then scanned the field for Jesse.

He was on his own thirty-yard line, crouched to receive the snap. Seventy yards to go. Not much chance of a touchdown, even if they did let him pass. The Gators were bunched to defend against the run, all right. Jesse faked a hand-off, eluded the only linebacker who wasn't drawn in by it, and passed to Hap. It was an easy fifty yards.

Betsy found herself yelling, "Yay, Jesse! That's the way!"

Tad was beside himself, leaping up and down and screaming himself hoarse along with most of the rest of the fans. The noise was deafening. On the giant screen at one end of the field the pass was being replayed, and Betsy could watch it this time without anxiety clawing at her stomach.

Above the chanting, cheering crowd, Jesse's larger-than-life figure took the snap, stepped fluidly back—three long steps, four more short ones—then skipped to the side, ducked under the outstretched arm of a defender, found Hap, stepped forward onto his left leg, and fired straight over the head of an onrushing mountain of man.

Betsy shook her head in admiration and relief.

"Isn't he something?" Alex asked in awe.

"He sure is," she said with feeling.

Jesse approached the sideline to get quick instructions from his coach. As if they'd planned it, Tad and Alex together cupped their hands around their mouths and yelled, "Jesse!"

He didn't seem to have heard them, listening intently to Coach Paulson. But just before he trotted back onto the field, he glanced up. Betsy waved, and Alex lifted his arm above her head to point down at her. Jesse's quick flash of recognition told Betsy he'd seen her. She sighed in relief.

"They're in position for a touchdown, now," Alex said, forgetting that Betsy knew more about the game than he did. "The Gators'll key on Jesse."

She had realized that and would have preferred not to have it pointed out.

Paulson called for a running play. With so many of the Gator defenders blitzing, Collins had a good inside path. He made it to the twenty-one-yard line. The fans' cheering hardly affected the noise level. They hadn't stopped yelling since the last play.

"Good," Betsy muttered. "Run it on in."

The gain wasn't enough for a first down, and it hadn't kept Jesse from being knocked flat by a lineman who couldn't or didn't want to stop his forward momentum when he saw that Kincaid didn't have the ball. Jesse picked himself up and hurried his teammates back to the line. They were playing against the clock now.

The next play was a pass, but there wasn't a lot of room for receivers to elude the coverage. Jesse danced, looking for a receiver. No one. He dodged a defender, still searching for a hole.

Betsy bit her lip so hard it bled. "Watch out!" she screamed as a burly linebacker shook off a Miner and hurled himself at Jesse.

They went down together, the linebacker landing full on Jesse's outstretched leg. In a momentary lull in the crowd roar, she thought she actually heard the bone snap. Her scream this time was pure anguish. "No!"

Jesse had his hands to his helmet. His head was thrown back and his mouth open in a grimace of terrible pain. The man who'd broken the leg was up, gesturing frantically to the Miner trainers. He was obviously horrified at what had happened.

For five seconds, Betsy thought she was going to faint. Then came the thought, *Jesse needs me.* With that, she was over the railing and around the bench onto the field, running toward Jesse, ten yards behind the trainers.

She was five feet away when a trainer saw her and grabbed at her coat. "Hold it, Miss! You can't—"

"Please!" she begged. "I have to see him."

The man was waving for a security guard. "Get her off the field!"

But Jesse had heard her. "Betsy!" he called from the ground. "Tom, let her through! She's my fiancée."

The trainer looked shocked. "Oh, sorry, ma'am. Go ahead."

Betsy was beside Jesse before permission was out of the man's mouth. "Jesse," she breathed in love and anguish, putting a hand to his cheek. His skin was pale and clammy, his pupils enlarged. She could tell by his breathing that he was in terrible pain, but he was smiling at her with delight in spite of it.

"You came," he said. He shook his head admiringly. "What a woman!"

"How is it?" she asked him. Her voice was calm, in spite of her inner turmoil.

"Hurts like hell," he admitted, "but I'll live."

His forehead and upper lip were beaded with perspiration. She wiped them with a gentle hand, smiling her love into his eyes. He reached for her hand and squeezed. "Don't let any photographers close to me on the way out if you can help it," he instructed her urgently.

"Nowhere near," she promised. She felt quite fierce, to her own surprise. She'd do some screeching if she had to.

The stretcher arrived, and the team doctor supervised the job of getting Jesse onto it. Betsy held his hand the whole time. She thought he was going to pass out from the pain, but his eyes cleared once he was settled and the truck began to move. The security guards were doing a good job controlling the crowd of cameramen and photographers, so Betsy could concentrate on Jesse.

Around them was clamor and hubbub. People shouted instructions, called questions, and ran to and fro, gesturing. Through it all, Betsy and Jesse focused on each other. Except when Jesse's eyes had closed in pain, they hadn't shifted off her. As they approached the ambulance, he said, "Well, it's one less worry for us. That's the end of my football career, finally."

Her momentary flash of gladness was overridden when she recognized the sadness he was trying to hide. He was in severe pain, and he was thinking that his team might be in the Super Bowl without him. He was thinking he was finished before he was ready to be. She couldn't be glad about something that he regretted so much. She'd come halfway, driving here like a madwoman, facing her fear to support him. Now she had to go the other half.

"Who are you kidding?" she asked him. "You'll be back. You're not through yet, and I'll be at every game from now on."

He stared at her, his eyes beginning to glaze from the pain-killing injection the doctor had administered. To make sure he understood, she added softly, "You'll quit next year, or when you're fifty. I don't want you to retire before you're ready." His grip on her hand grew stronger as his eyes closed on a long exhalation. She couldn't be sure, but she thought there was relief as well as pain in that sigh.

Attendants were waiting to slide his stretcher into the ambulance. They busied themselves about him with straps and hoists. She stared at his pale face, realizing with a lift of the heart that what she'd said was true. It wasn't just a panacea for Jesse.

She couldn't diminish him by letting her fears influence him into giving in to this injury. Life was risk. It was better to get hurt than to live in constriction and fear. She'd taken a chance on loving him and she had to let him take his chances on the football field or wherever he chose. Together they'd handle it.

Just before he was shifted into the ambulance and their grip broken, she said, "The only problem we're going to have is figuring out how to make love with you in traction."

She knew he'd heard her. Nothing else could explain the little smile that made a man with a fractured leg look happy and completely at peace.

THE EDITOR'S CORNER

Seven is supposed to be a lucky number . . . so look for luck next month as you plunge into the four delightful LOVESWEPT romances and the second trilogy of the Delaney series. Has the Free Sampler of **THE DELANEYS OF KILLAROO** made you eager to read the full books? (Whenever we do a book sampler I get the most wonderful letters of protest! Many of them very funny.) As you know from the creative promotion we've done with Clairol® to help them launch their new product, PAZAZZ® SHEER COLORWASH will be available next month when the Delaney books, too, are out. Think how much fun it would be to do your own personal make-over in the style of one of the heroines of **THE DELANEYS OF KILLAROO**! *Adelaide, The Enchantress* by Kay Hooper has hair like *Sheer Fire; Matilda, The Adventuress* by Iris Johansen has tresses with the spicy allure of *Sheer Cinnamon; Sydney, The Temptress* by Fayrene Preston has a mystery about her echoed in the depths of her *Sheer Plum* hair color. Enjoy this big three!

And for your four LOVESWEPTS, you start with **A DREAM TO CLING TO,** LOVESWEPT #206. Sally Goldenbaum makes her debut here as a solo author— you'll remember Sally has teamed up in the past with Adrienne Staff—and has created a love story that is filled with tenderness and humor and great passion. Brittany Winters is a generous, spirited woman who believes life should be taken seriously. This belief immediately puts her at odds with the roguishly handsome Sam Lawrence, originator of "Creative Games." Sam is a wanderer, a chaser of dreams . . .

(continued)

and a man who is utterly irresistible. (What woman could resist a man who calls her at dawn and tells her to watch the sunrise while he whispers words of love to her?) **A DREAM TO CLING TO** is an enchanting book that we think you will remember for a long time.

PLAYING HARD TO GET, LOVESWEPT #207, is one of Barbara Boswell's most intriguing stories yet. Slade Ramsey is the proverbial nice guy, but, jilted by his fiancee, he got tired of finishing last. Figuring women really did prefer scoundrels, he tried hard to become one. However, he was only playing the part of a charming heartbreaker, and he never got over the love he felt for the first woman he had treated badly—young and innocent Shavonne Brady. When he comes face to face with Shavonne, gazing again into her big brown eyes and seeing the woman she has become, Slade knows he can never leave her again. But how can he convince her that the man she knew a few years ago—the one who had broken her heart—isn't the real Slade? Barbara has written a truly memorable story, and not only will you fall in love with Shavonne and Slade, but all of their brothers and sisters are unforgettable characters as well.

In **KATIE'S HERO** by Kathleen Creighton, LOVE-SWEPT #208, Katherine Taylor Winslow comes face to face with Hollywood's last swashbuckling star, Cole Grayson. Katie is a writer who always falls in love with the heroes of her novels. Now she's doing a biography of Cole . . . and he's the epitome of a hero. How can she fail to fall for him? Katie and her hero are as funny and warmhearted a pair as you're ever likely to find in a romance, and we think you are going to be as amused by Katie as a tenderfoot on Cole's ranch as

(continued)

you are beguiled by the tenderness of a hero who's all man. This book is a real treat!

Only Sara Orwig could turn a shipwreck into a romantic meeting, and she does just that in **VISIONS OF JASMINE,** LOVESWEPT #209. After the ship she and her fellow researchers were on sinks, Jasmine Kirby becomes separated from her friends, alone in her own lifeboat. She is thrilled when she is rescued, but a little dubious about the rescuer—a scruffy sailor with a hunk's body and a glint in his eye that warns her to watch out for her virtue. Matthew Rome is bewitched by Jasmine, and begins to teach her how to kick up her heels and live recklessly. When they meet again in Texas, Jasmine is astounded to discover that the man she'd thought was a charming ne'er do well actually lives a secret and dangerous life.

Four great LOVESWEPTs and three great Delaney Dynasty novels . . . a big Lucky Seven just for you next month.

With every good wish,

Sincerely,

Carolyn Nichols

Carolyn Nichols
  Editor
LOVESWEPT
Bantam Books, Inc.
666 Fifth Avenue
New York, NY 10103

It's a little like being Loveswept

SHEER MADNESS

SHEER COLOR

SHEER PASSION

SHEER EXCITEMENT

SHEER INTRIGUE

SHEER ROMANCE

All it takes is a little imagination and more Pazazz.®

Coming this July from Clairol…Pazazz Sheer Color Wash —8 inspiring sheer washes of color that last up to 4 shampoos.

Look for the Free Loveswept *THE DELANEYS OF KILLAROO* book sampler this July in participating stores carrying Pazazz Sheer Color Wash.

 **LOVESWEPT**

Love Stories you'll never forget by authors you'll always remember

☐	21795	**Where The Heart Is #174** Eugenia Riley	$2.50
☐	21796	**Expose #175** Kimberli Wagner	$2.50
☐	21794	**'Til The End Of Time #176** Iris Johansen	$2.50
☐	21802	**Hard Habit To Break #177** Linda Cajio	$2.50
☐	21807	**Disturbing The Peace #178** Peggy Webb	$2.50
☐	21801	**Kaleidoscope #179** Joan Elliott Pickart	$2.50
☐	21797	**The Dragon Slayer #180** Patt Bucheister	$2.50
☐	21790	**Robin And Her Merry People #181** Fayrene Preston	$2.50
☐	21756	**Makin' Whoopee #182** Billie Green	$2.50
☐	21811	**Tangles #183** Barbara Boswell	$2.50
☐	21812	**Sultry Nights #184** Anne Kolaczyk & Ed Kolaczyk	$2.50
☐	21809	**Sunny Chandler's Return #185**	$2.50
☐	21810	**Fiddlin' Fool #186** Susan Richardson	$2.50
☐	21814	**Last Bridge Home #187** Iris Johansen	$2.50
☐	21822	**Detour To Euphoria #188** Becky Lee Weyrich	$2.50
☐	21798	**In Serena's Web #189** Kay Hooper	$2.50
☐	21823	**Wild Poppies #190** Joan Elliott Pickart	$2.50
☐	21828	**Across the River of Yesterday #191** Iris Johansen	$2.50
☐	21813	**The Joy Bus #192** Peggy Webb	$2.50
☐	21824	**Raven On the Wing #193** Kay Hooper	$2.50
☐	21829	**Not A Marrying Man #194** Barbara Boswell	$2.50
☐	21825	**Wind Warning #195** Sara Orwig	$2.50
☐	21771	**Solid Gold Prospect #196** Hertha Schulze	$2.50

Prices and availability subject to change without notice.

Buy them at your local bookstore or use this handy coupon for ordering: